SHINY

Rudy Wilson

1st WORLD
PUBLISHING

Shiny

Rudy Wilson

Copyright © 2014 Rudy Wilson

Published by Inkfingerz
A Division of 1st World Publishing
P.O. Box 2211, Fairfield, Iowa 52556
tel: 641-209-5000 • fax: 866-440-5234
web: www.1stworldpublishing.com

First Edition

LCCN: 2014937534
SoftCover ISBN: 978-1-4218-8689-3
HardCover ISBN: 978-1-4218-8690-9
eBook ISBN: 978-1-4218-8691-6

This material has been written and published for educational purposes to enhance one's well-being. In regard to health issues, the information is not intended as a substitute for appropriate care and advice from health professionals, nor does it equate to the assumption of medical or any other form of liability on the part of the publisher or author. The publisher and author shall have neither liability nor responsibility to any person or entity with respect to loss, damages, or injury claimed to be caused directly or indirectly by any information in this book.

To Julie, with love, and to my mentor, Gordon Lish.

BOOK 1

PROLOUGE

An Early Memory

Elizabeth Apalaris
Miss Shirley - 8th Grade
April 11, 1963

I am like someone in a snapshot, found by a stranger who sees me, and thinks, "Who's that?" That's how I feel about me. I don't think I always did, feel that way.

I remember an egg, hardboiled, back then, a very early memory to me. I was a little girl. I sat across from my brother Carl at the breakfast table. He said I should just hide it in my mouth, from my mother, cause I didn't want to eat it. Mother said I had to eat it. So I hid it in my cheek.

I kept the egg in my cheek all the way to school, in school, during lunch, where I ate on the other side of my mouth, and drank my milk. I kept the egg in my mouth for the rest of the day, on the way home, and at swimming practice. For the whole day.

Carl knew and told my mom, and she laughed, and got mad and laughed again.

When I was twelve some boys pushed me down and buried me in a shallow grave. They called it that. They said "death to Shiny." My brother Carl was there. He hid from me. He showed away his eyes.

They touched me. They were "preoccupied" with my face.

My Mom killed herself with a gun when I was thirteen. When she found out about Carl, and those boys, and after a bad phone conversation with my dad, she died. They held me down and bled on my face, and they stood above me and did it down onto me. They covered me with dirt and their stuff, and they laughed. My brother hid behind them. He never did it. He always liked me alot. He watched me from our second floor window, from my room, while I sang. I sang to him, outside while he watched me.

He slept with me in my bed. He kissed my whole body. We swam in the early mornings in the Gordon's pond. He washed me. We broke God's heart because we were brother and sister and my mother killed herself with a gun, in the head. She called Dodie, our neighbor and told her what we did. She laughed about the egg, and didn't laugh later about me. My Dad was gone by then, for good. My mom and me and Carl lived to-gether after he left us.

I rode a bus out of town after I had to leave for good. A free ride. I had a suitcase and my Brownie camera on its strap. I took a picture of our old house and my bicycle they said I would get later. I took a picture of my face to send to Carl, but later when it came out they said they would not send it to him, to forget him for now.

I promised him I would always think about him. I told him to picture me in every way, each sideways, top and bottom, and I would step in and fill in the picture in his mind. He had a big head. I have felt it when it got up, heated up over me. He was a good boy, he had a rough face on his skin, but such nice eyes that were more alive, and yet scared. He loved me with passion. On the bus I imagined him. I held his hand. It was like a needle. *Carl, I will always be Shiny*, I thought.

On the dead, old bus, I was pushed all the way to a dirty town to live in, in Cleveland. The wind blows dirt in your face here and dirties a white blouse.

I would not swallow that egg.

I cut my hand on a fence watching Carl be walked away.

I drew him on my bus magazine. I tired not to cry, but then I did.

It probably wasn't that bad what the boys did. I know more now about it. They raped me, on the outside. I knew they would. I don't hate them. They probably don't remember. Carl chased home after me.

There were five stop signs down at the Point where we used to live. When I had my hair newly cut, I liked it when it got along my face and in front of my eyes. I could make out the five red shapes, and I squinted to make them blur, to make them mine. They last longer that way.

My real name is Elizabeth.

That's what they called me in my new home. I kept Shiny hidden away. They are old and too quiet where I live. I'd rather have the boys and the dirt hole they put me in. If I have to live here alone and in a deep quiet, I'll die from it.

The only thing that was beautiful about that day was that while they were kissing me and doing it, I saw my red coat on the ground someone had thrown there. I stared at it the whole time I could. It was so red. I loved it, and the red got in my eyes. Then they picked it up, and brought it over and covered me up with it.

That was an Early Memory. Now I am a girl in a school who thinks mostly about the past. I don't ever think about now, and the future is filled with the same past and faces that I miss.

The End

CHAPTER 1

They took Shiny away from me, on a morning in 1959. I never saw her again.

It was because of what I did with her, and to her, once, in the small world we made. And our mother died of it. Then there was just me, left to think about her from then on.

Shiny cut her hand, holding to the sharp, wooden fence post when she saw me taken away. She watched me for a long time. And still, she watches. I was her older brother, once good. Her...she was the best. She was my sister.

I still see the little cut on her hand. It was like her colors, the red ones. She put all these separate red ones into a big crayon box, together on her shelf, with her collection of elves, angels and faeries, a picture of Dad, and said redcolors: *like the blood of her child's heart, of our one wrong-heart that beat always together...and still does...*

She stared at me one morning at the breakfast table. Her feet just touched the floor. I look now to see, to remember. Her hands... I could see them both. One rested flat, curled some, now that I thought of it, there on the table.

Her eyes glassed up. Her straight hair was cut, even, down to just below her chin. As she watched me, I put down my fork. I couldn't eat. I felt bad, but tender, like when there's fever.

Shiny cried about me.

"What's the matter with you two?" my mother asked us.

"I don't know," I said. "There's something here. Something I see."

"Tell me," she said. "What is it, Carl? Tell me."

My mother leaned over to me. Shiny held her fork in the air, in her thin hand.

"A man," I said. "By himself. Walking in the night time. He's not happy; he's sad."

"Who is it?" she asked.

"It's me," I told her. "It has to be me!"

Shiny yelled across the table to me, "Am I there! Am I there with you?"

"No," I told her. "I don't know where you are -"

Then she had a lonely mouth.

Me and Shiny: what we were, we were, without then knowing what, or even really when, and certainly never why.

CHAPTER 2

My little house, where I sat now, and thought of Shiny, from twenty-five years, was brick-wooden, with two doors, on either end. One was never opened, and so the bushes and vines grew all over it. It could be opened, but never was. I had to try it, and it was hard, and dirt-filled the room, messy. It was the police that made me do it, out in the view and sunshine of everyone.

My house smelled of smoke, from burning paper in the bathroom. I spent the morning on the bathroom floor, looking through cardboard boxes. I squinted to see my old handwriting, and to remember the years.

Out in front of the regular front door, was someone's back yard nearby, hedged in by a row of bushes. In them was a crawl-through hole where the kids got through, to go between the yards.

I watched that place sometimes out my window. And at night I looked at it. I wanted to use it and be a part of it, its entrance to somewhere else to be.

Some policemen came and knocked on my door. They knocked hard and said who they were. I thought of the crawl-place, and the back door I had. I got up and threw on some pants, shoes, and a shirt. I forced open the door. Dirt fell in, and wild green pushed in at me. I got out and into the thick. It was a wide, big yard behind me. I went out. I could have run away.

Slowly, I went over to the side of the house and watched the police, two of them, standing at the mat on the front step, a piece of carpet, old, and worn. They stood and waited in the morning air. When they saw me they asked me if I was Carl Apalaris, and I said that yes, I was.

"I am, for now," I said. "Who are you guys?"

They said they were the police. They had names that were like Witherspoon and Indiana. They arrested me for window breaking, for destruction of private property.

I said I didn't know what to say.

They said I didn't have to say anything at all.

I knew I broke down a door, and broke some windows. The moon had shined on them. I saw that. Then when they broke I still saw it, jagged, slanty, reflected there still. I saw myself there too, wild, and not like me.

I ran away. I was scared. I had loved a woman, and had done that. She was married to someone there. He hurt her, his lonesome wife, and I had been there to see it. So, I hit the glass.

I locked the house, and while I was inside I took a quick look out the window at the crawl hole. It was there. In the car, as we passed it, I tried not to see it. I looked away. I felt small in the back seat. I leaned into the corner. I didn't want to see it, riding with them in a car.

In the blue car we rolled slowly over towards the jail. I was going to jail. There would be the narrow slit of a window, facing out to the street.

Light came in it, but you couldn't see out of it. It was serious glass. It made me a prisoner; it denied me.

"You were easy to find, Carl. Real easy –"

"I know," I said. "I don't care."

"You're in for it, you know," said one cop.

I took glass from his cut hand, the last time. He got some of it. I helped him when I could have run. I broke more of Joey's husband's windows this time. Now he looked at me. "This time, I can't help you much."

"It's alright," I said.

I remembered what someone had said about me. I sat littler in the car. Someone I knew. I hardly knew anyone in this town. I lived in the dark side of it. I knew its night face. She said to me: "I saw you the other night, in your house. I was walking by, and it made me so sad."

"Sad?" I asked her. "Why sad? The house? It is the lowest in town, I guess." Now, leaving it, I felt a love for it, for its ugliness, and how it held itself up – it didn't know; it held itself as well as it could.

"No," she said. "Not that. I saw you through the window, cause the light was on. I could see an outline of you. You were standing up, by yourself; you were leaning against something, at a strange angle. It just made me feel sad."

I turned now to look back at it, but we were too far away. I lived there for years. No one visited much. A girl named Cokie had, some. She never judged me.

* * *

The past many years were a black-out, they were cut out shapes. There was a small school picture of a boy I knew. He was a dishwasher in town; he was so shy. His picture was stuck in a mirror, and in it he was an adolescent, and he had that look, awkward, and sad, and trying, and with a knowing, about pain, the pain of the young. And he knew it would never lessen. He wore glasses, he had a frozen smile. I joked with him sometimes. He watched me once as I walked away, for several blocks. It made me feel terrible.

We passed a dead squirrel on its side. I looked at the back of his head; it was silent. He looked like he was asleep in a little bed. But he was smashed dead in the street.

I couldn't see the cops anymore. A shape was coming in my eyes. It got blurry, that shape I could never escape. Why did I only see the sad? I tried not to, but there was only that pain.

Where was Shiny? I never, never should have told anyone about her. Never. Did she go through adolescence that way, like I did? Was she sad?

I heard, "... and you're on a thirty day suspended sentence already, you know."

I couldn't see them anymore, only feel them out there. I could hear. I never should have said a thing about her, about what happened.

We curved in and parked. I wanted everything to turn red, or any color, an all-over color: us, the car, the lot, the jail, that slit window, the air, and the Earth. I could walk away, I could be alone. I'd see Shiny riding her bike through it all. I'd run after her in the one color. She couldn't ride a bike that well. She wouldn't ride it down the big hills.

When I walked to the station door between the two men, I thought of her. I slowed, I resisted the door. I thought of my sister. I thought about Shiny:

The Point was a place we walked to when we were little, a place where five streets came together at one point. It was near our house. There was a drugstore there. It was called The Point, too. We looked at stuff inside, through the window. I held Shiny's hand. It was small. I loved her. I only hurt her one time; it was them, at her heart.

Shiny.

We moved away from The Point.

Then after Mom fell, we lived our lives separate. Shiny was in a corner all day, watching me watch the shape that came out of Mother's head.

I always see her backed into that nice corner. There was wallpaper; it was pretty.

Shiny sat, and watched, and she listened, but she never got close enough but once, to know the shape. I took her by the hand, and she closed her eyes. I guided her face to the spot where she could kiss, one last time, her mother's lips.

* * *

The reason I was in jail, or was supposed to be, was because of the glass. It was marked by a small, painful X shaped scar on the palm of my hand – and the pain spread out too. And when the policeman picked me up that first time, he fell, into the glass of the window I had smashed. I broke them, where Joey lived. I helped him take out a large piece. It wasn't him that had done it, had hurt. It was a woman, and it was her husband's glass all over the house, and it spilled all over the yard, where we found ourselves. When I looked in his palm for the glass, in the dark, it took on the shape, and it got big, much, much bigger than me, or my mind, even. I felt like a tiny, gripping thing, holding to a piece of glass as big as Texas, almost infinite then, like from a deep forever, when the little things, like a thumb, become huge, unimaginably large, and windy.

* * *

For part of a day, the three of us were in that room, Shiny in the corner, and me very near – and at times completely absorbed in that shape on the floor. The three of us were quieter than ever before, than it ever could be again, as quiet as my mother, without any breath.

In that silent triangle, a friend of my mother's came in, walked in, and saw us. In a nice room, turned, changed, and holding, in the only way that we could, in our positions: our dear mother, who died over us: me at fourteen, and Shiny, she was only and forever thirteen.

I heard the woman say something about a *tragedy*, and I had a smile growing, not from me, but from the shape that had its own life and loved the taking over of my own.

Shiny's real name was something like Elizabeth.

I could smell something, now, like wax. I thought of how wax was, how it could be shaped into anything. I had the fear crawling.

"This way, boy – you know the way, I believe." It was the policeman with the same scar on his hand as I had, shared. They called me a boy.

"What's in your pockets?" they asked. "Empty them."

I was almost a forty year old boy.

"Nothing," I said. "I have nothing."

"Let's have it all. And your belt, and your shoelaces."

"I'm not going to kill myself –"

"Well, we have to be sure. And we – we're not too sure about you, Carl."

"Well," I said. "Well." We were in a little room, sectioned off. I pulled away. They held my wrists. "Don't," I said. "You're not sure," I said, "not sure..."

"Carl," they said. They pulled my hands, on my wrists, tighter. I could make out the shape between us all, how it was, how it moved, how it mocked me, and them not seeing it anywhere, how it danced.

"Don't take my watch," I said.

"It doesn't even look like it works," they said.

"It doesn't. It was my little sister's, a long time ago. I put it on when I saw you guys pull up at my house. I had it in a box."

"An old one, huh?"

"Yes. She was a little girl, but she wore this anyway. It's got a neat band, too - the same one. I got it out to wear cause I might be in here for a long time. Can't I?"

"Yeah, go ahead. Go on with it. Don't cut yourself up with it."

"I won't. Not with Shiny's watch."

"That her name?"

"I hope so," I said.

There had been a year, many years ago, when my mother's death caught up with me. It was all I could see.

"Okay," they said, "sign here – on the dotted line, for your things."

I kept seeing things in a certain way. I kept seeing just that part of whatever there was to see, the part that looked like the shape.

They walked me down to my cell. I started to tell them about it: "...and even if I was looking straight at you, it's what I saw – it's all I saw, that shape, a thing in itself – it wanted to take me over, and I –"

And they closed the outer door to the cell and left me alone. I turned into the corner, standing. I lowered my voice: "– but it got in the way. It was around the time I heard about where Shiny was. They wouldn't tell me about her, just an address where she'd been kept all those years – it wouldn't let me go there to her."

I heard my own whispering: "...it took me over." I found out an amazing thing, amazing: "I became it."

I talked quietly to the corner where two cement walls met – "And it became me. It's all I was. I wasn't Carl anymore."

I had new borders, a new color, a new name.

I pushed myself into the corner. I always saw the red color of it, the blood-color, its power, of what it was to me, and Shiny over in her corner, away from it, where she lived the rest of my life.

"Shiny," I said, "forgive me, please." I felt her small hands. Her fingers spelled out her name. "Shiny, where are you? I'm sorry for what I did."

I made her want to cry; I made Shiny go away.

"I spent that year without you," I said. I leaned down in the corner, low near the floor. It was dark, quiet. There was the one, slit window.

* * *

My mother's death had a shape like a jagged lake. It was cold, It got mean, It was laughing at me, sometimes pretty though, and sometimes terrible, but always mine. I was a frozen, warm lake in a hospital for a year.

I didn't hear one word. I didn't see, or touch, or imagine. Maybe the lake had red-blood thoughts, but I didn't know them.

"Shiny, you were outside it. At a far distance, you were watching. It was all a memory. I guess it's all a memory, everything.

"No wind blew on the lake. It was stuck."

Now I could feel the cool cement on my face. I had ended up here. I felt for her, for IT, we three, Shiny, and me, and the lake that came from my mother's death. We all came from her. Three: Father, Son, and Holy Ghost in a blood lake.

My mother – *a Mother can never deny the Son* – I asked her there, on the floor of the cell, "Please mother, forgive me. Send Shiny back to me."

CHAPTER 3

Mother always felt like ginger, like thin, see-through lace. She rode a high, high, tight wire. Her head came off all the time.

Me and Shiny, we took care of her. We petted her to sleep most nights, after Daddy left. I was scared by a horse story she told. A story about the grandfather I never met. What did it take to make a horse, or a child?

"Mommy, it's okay," said Shiny. "It's okay, don't cry. Don't always cry."

I felt her thick hair, lying down, and her whiskey breath that reminded me of the English, hand-made cabinet she inherited and used as a bar, out in the hallway. "It's a hallway piece" – dark hallway to creep through alone at night. It was where she was from, England, brought over, a little girl herself then, and her father in the story she told was dead from a horse he loved. The horse kicked him into a box, and they were put into the grave together as one. She'd smile in her drink and in her broken looking teeth.

Shiny was bright, such a bright. She jumped over a dead horse, on roller skates.

"Shiny." I was falling down again, going under the color that my mother made.

"I don't want to live, so alone, but..." and I drifted down

under the lake, "... I'll sleep, and there'll be a fragile dream to keep me."

* * *

My mother, like a leaf; she was paper-thin. I kissed her, too, when she was dead. Dead-happier.

"Didn't you know?" Shiny said, "not to? Didn't you know how Mom is? Did you see her face?" Did Shiny know we'd never see each other again?

"Didn't you know what would happen to us?"

My sister was obsessed with her face. She had a problem with mirrors. She wasn't stuck-up on her bright, because she was that; she pushed and pulled at it, and cried at it. She hid it. Shiny hid all the mirrors in the house.

"People look at me and they read my face," she said. "Wrong."

People saw her light. She smeared red all over the big mirror in the hall near the old, wooden bar. More than once she broke all the small, hand held ones. She broke them and then looked at herself in the pieces.

"I hate it," she sobbed. "I hate my stupid face. I feel how everybody stares at it. The tiniest thing makes it stick out. It's too big, and ugly!"

And beautiful, like her name, and like how she spoke to me, and petted her mother to sleep, and was little, and hiding. She was like a little girl who would never grow past this awful point.

carl put a hole in his mother's head, no, i did not, did i, shiny, did i? you were there – did i? does she live now somewhere hidden behind gauzy veils? is she old with a garden to hide her face in?

is she a little girl, still? is she also near forty years, is her face mostly always red? isn't she my only and needed mother, lost to me? lost to a shape i never wanted, or planned to see. did i, as a baby, or before, somehow plan to have a whole life dominated and slanted and ruined by a shape in red, spilled out, squeezed out of a

*head onto the floor of a house, a place where people lived together,
not knowing? i didn't plan that, i never saw myself laid out in a
field sniffed by dogs, chased by a shape. i'd planned to grow into a
person.*

But when Shiny cried, she rushed to get her hidden hand
mirror. She had one with red glass rubies all along the back of
it: Shiny, my sister. She looked in it and cried harder. "See,"
she'd say, "See!"

Before they took us away, separated us into foster homes, I
had to come back to get some things, alone, without her, with
other people, and I saw her bike, out, leaned against the side of
the house, being rained on.

I tied her bike up to the power meter that came out of the
ground. She'd have to think about me when she spent her time
untying it. I held her, and I rode sometimes with her when we
lived together, when we were a boy and a girl.

I watched her in the tub. She said not to. It was the best
place to talk, and the water made the room get hot with steam.
She shook the water so I wouldn't look in and see her. She sat
on her self, naked, on pink porcelain. On the tub surface sat a
child with my heart.

She slapped her face and poked her mouth out when it hurt
her to do it. I never hit her there. Some boys more than touched
her face; it scared her, not believing it could happen. Blood,
and a deeper white-blood, that smelled like a distant world
she didn't want to know of yet. Boys, that howled, and leaned
back, curved, and then down at her, on her. And dirt piled on
her shiny face. And me, that was letting, and letting.

* * *

"Shiny," I heard. I held my hands, my arms around my
head in a circle, on the flat mat in the little jail cell I had all by

myself. When I got up to get water from the white porcelain bowl, I thought – 'her water in my mouth. What did things taste like now in her mouth?'

The thought: *rain on Shiny's bike.*

It reminded me. One time, I felt like a man. It had been raining. I was thirteen. Shiny would be eleven. I knew all about Shiny, her age, her days and nights, her face, where she was, and who. I felt a quickening about all of Shiny's facts.

I knew her classroom, her teacher, and how people watched her. I saw them do it. I knew she was four feet eleven inches tall. She weighed eighty-three pounds. I knew how her eyes could get dark, and darker, and knowing, and get back in when she found out secret things. How she watched Mother's nakedness once from behind her, and me watching her. It was always us three. It was always secret about what was so obvious: that we loved each other, and that we liked each other, and that we lived in and floated for years in a house by ourselves, like a scared and sacred box with a light on in it; a life raft, and a girl who grew up without me, and could have even died.

I watched Shiny's naked back, too, while she stood looking out the window. It was an early, yellow morning, and blued. Shiny's naked, white back, her shoulder blades piercing the air in her bedroom.

So it was me watching her being half-naked watching out, and that other time watching Mother, naked, and me, remembered as crouching down in a half-open doorway. I could've gone in and said to them both, them being almost twin-like in their white skins, in being pretty, mother the whitest, and said, "Say, can I see you like this? Am I part of you both? Do I have a place to live in? Can I? Can I be here and feel okay about seeing you and knowing you like you really are, Mother, or do I have to pretend to be a child all my life long without you both?"

* * *

Shiny saw me at school that one time, out the fifth grade window, all covered in paper cut-outs, stickers, orange and black, and Halloween, black cats, and fresh clear air to see Shiny in. She must've seen me out there with the pole. I crossed the younger children in. Shiny slid her hand along it when she passed. She opened her mouth. The pole had a flag on it. It flapped in the time that I was there, and young. It made a wave of red color.

It was raining that day. I was captain, and had a badge, and a strap that came across and over my heart. I folded it a certain way at night, to keep until morning came: and what the nights held in between, me and her in the same house.

Shiny was like a tree in our backyard. It'll still be there now. It was like her waist. Shiny had a waist and a chest and a face that got ruined and hurt, and cast a shadow on my mother's grave.

I had dark hair, blacker from the rain. I liked it to be wet like that, and as I walked down the hall, my half-moon heel taps clicked. Shiny was with a friend and when I walked by, I heard her voice say, "That's my brother," and she half-pointed, gestured with her hand, with her whole body at me.

Her soul was mixed up with mine. Even with the blood that got into her child's mouth, and white-blood.

She let her straight brown hair fall down along the sides of her face. She felt best when it was like that; it held her face like thin hands. I liked how it separated into strands, long and sweet, into pieces hanging down.

It moved when she did, and when she was very still, her head bent over and down, to draw, or write, it hung more over her face. It sometimes touched the paper, or the table, that way. Her lips were thick, and sometimes it's all I could see, her red lips, and chin, and the strands, the room reaching twilight. I could hear the soft scratching of her pen or her gliding colored crayons across the empty white paper.

* * *

Once I asked her why there were cats and dogs here, on earth with us.

"There are dogs to dig holes and there are cats to be run over by cars and lie there with sad, dead cat faces on in the middle of the road. Also there are cats to look at birds, especially gray cats. They will all look like gray cats in the dark. There are yellow dogs so that they can eat corncobs.

"They fill up space that might otherwise be taken up with things like truck tires and beer and bad Dad-cologne smells.

"Five cats fill the space of one bad cologne.

"Ten dogs fill the space of fifty dead pigeons. Dogs are nicer than dead pigeons.

"It's just arithmetic: one dog erases one shower that won't work very well and keeps making the water too hot to take a shower in. Fifty cats erase one day of a boy in a poor place eating dirt and bad food, maybe even the whole boy, if the cats are good enough…but fifty scabs eaten by a very hungry boy — erases one good cat, so you have to be careful." She didn't smile or anything when she said things this way, just all non-chalant and throw-away.

When they put her in the ground, like a shallow, early grave, she fought it, but they held her. I never touched her. She didn't say then, "That's my brother, there." She didn't half point; she screamed. I could have saved her. I could have helped her up.

I did, too late. I followed her home. She was limping. I ran behind her, just us two, now. But she wouldn't let me touch her. I tried to touch her back, her shoulder, in a blue shirt, all dirtied, but she said, "No, don't!"

In my bed that night, before the morning when my mother died, I gripped the covers with my fists. It was pitch black. Shiny'd run in the back kitchen door. I remembered her angle, jumping into the house like it was a bowl, her legs cutting fast to the side, pushing her through the house and up the short stairs to the hallway to her room. Then she slammed herself in the bathroom where the mirror was.

In the pitch black, I saw her face clearly. Red blood, and dirt, and smeary. Shiny's thin arms and legs, and a dress and a blue blouse, and her heart wrapped up in it, and me and her like a dance, and Mother downstairs like a drawing in a light blue crayon done by Shiny, easy to erase.

She came into my room, and kneeled down by my bed. She laid her forehead by my knees, at that place, at that level, away from where I was.

"Why, Carl, why did they do it to me?" She broke out a small cry, a small sound like she was under water. "I think I could've taken it on my back, but not on my front. They put dirt on me, Carl, and they bled, and stuff." Her voice got smaller, trailed. "Did you, too, Carl? Did you? I was upside down, it's scary to remember, oh it's so scary. Why did they touch me like that? Did they have to?"

She never pressed me if I did that to her. She saw me as I hid from her eyes, and from the others, behind them, but watching, and letting, and from then on, to be the least.

"Is it cause they hate me? Cause they hate my face, like I do?"

She hated to close her eyes; she felt people watching her, and thought they'd laugh if she wasn't aware. She had them closed when our father held her chin and mouth in one hand and squeezed her tears out. He said to her, to Shiny - but he never called her that – "You're not pretty like you think you are, like people say you are. Not to me. You're a poison-faced girl, just like your mother, but she's the worst. I am sick of looking at you and your faces."

I wanted and I waited, to kill him for that, for doing that, for ruining Shiny and her heart, which I ruined too, because she was so very, very beautiful to see.

"Shiny," I said. She climbed in; I helped her into my single bed, pulling her up by one arm. She got in and slept warm against me, with her face against my chest, on my side, down under my arm. She pressed in close to me. I held my arm around her. Her face was hidden, and safe, and healing. Maybe she dreamt of it being peeled away, like wax, for another one, an easier one to wear that wasn't so wonderful, and so bright, and so smeared by what animals were, and what a cruelty it became for a few to stand in a circle above her, and be male, on one afternoon, so they could live and be safer in the knowing that they had smeared a perfect birth.

* * *

Shiny never, never wanted to get up out of that bed again, that next morning, after, and neither did I.

My mother shot herself in her head the next day, after we were called down the short, wooden staircase to eat a breakfast that would sit uneaten for a day on the table from where my mother got up, and talked, and listened on the phone. She turned white, she lost the last strength. The upper part of her body seemed to fall. Her hair frizzed out some, breaking.

I tried to look away and never see her face turn, turn to see my own, about Shiny.

Later – she never said a word to either of us. Didn't she know, like we knew, how we were together as one thing, tied to each other, through each other, knotted together, lonesome, and were all we had? She never talked to me or Shiny again.

She burst into the living room like she came through a white wall. She filled it up. She had a small hand, like a girl. Her finger pulled a trigger and blew her away from us.

Shiny laughed a cry-laugh, a short, hopped scream at the sound. My heart got so little. The bullet might've gone through the whole house and landed out in the yard.

We waited, at the table, with spoons in our hands. We waited some more, a short, very small while. Then we jumped. We ran through the entrance space together, our shoulders scraping the sides, and we saw her, our eyes seeing at the same time. We knew her. We'd known her until now. Now we didn't anymore. And that's when Shiny, right then, went into the corner, squatting down, and later dropped to her knees. Sometimes, her eyes went up into her head, and I could see the whites of them.

I only lifted her head up once, to see, it not wanting me to. I saw where the blood pumped out. It pumped out of her head. I held my shirt to it, but it didn't do any good. Then, later, it stopped, and I guessed all of it, from her, was out on the rug. That's when I became who I am, and without her and Shiny anymore, and old, and with that shape inside me.

I put that day, my mother, far away, and tiny, almost unable to recall her as a person, a woman, a fragile, frightened lady.

I watched Shiny watching her, and then had to help her, her eyes closed, to find her mother's lips.

Maybe there was no Shiny anymore, anywhere, but maybe, maybe someone knows her, or someone at least very much like her.

CHAPTER 4

I recalled a closer time, a night, just a short time ago. It was me, what I had come to, without her. There had been such drunken clarity. It had been the start of something.

I was still me, in a small town's very edge, before it would disappear into the dark, in a late night, well-lit supermarket. I loved the pretty.

The colors were so bright; the floors were waxed, hard. They reflected the colors there. I was thinking of a lost time, of a pier, a Pepsi-Cola machine, blue and red, and how its colors waved and blurred in the river light. Shiny was there, in it; her legs hung down, disappearing into the night water.

There were only a few people here, in the store with me. Their eyes looked too little, or too big. They didn't speak. They watched. A man looked at a magazine. He held it; he looked past it at the floor.

I looked at the bottles of wine in the cooler. I found a long stick outside. I hit with it, the ground, the empty streets, at the air, and myself. I spelled out a name with it, in hits.

Twenty-five years had gone by. Where had she gone? Where was my sister Shiny, now?

I lingered in the aisles, where the colors were, from the boxes, from the bags along the shelves. They were gifts; they sat in their splendid.

Some cans fell down to the floor. I looked down at them. I moved on, slowly, hearing a voice that must have been my own. I felt cold, everywhere. I was a falling drunk. I fell on the floor, and then someone had me by the arm. "I'm sorry," I heard my voice say, "forgive me."

I saw my face in the window; it never got tired of betraying me. Me, in me for so long, left there. Somewhere, some time, it had been better… better, almost normal.

I saw somebody, a girl I knew, waiting for me. She leaned. She smelled like weeds, and dirt, outside, in her shoes broken down. She was young, and she had followed me before.

"You look like you've always been here," I said to her. "I was expecting someone here, someone."

"Me, too," said the girl.

"Wanna go for a ride?" she asked. She was slight and windy.

"I'll go," I said. "I had a broken thing here, I – I left it somewhere."

I searched my pockets and the floor around me, but forgot what for. I saw the way the girl's shirt stuck out in front, and hung out some above her thin-skinny waist from above it. "There," I said. I pointed at her with my eyes. She looked down at herself. I remembered the shinning, hard floor. My head felt a popping sound.

"You look so familiar to me," I said to her, in her shirt, in her blonde, falling hair. It was dirty.

"You look like me," I said. "Like a bad day –"

She looked back at me, so closely.

"I don't know why," I said.

"Carl – come for a ride. I'll take you. I've been looking for you."

"Why?"

"I want to talk with you, and hear you. There's good sounds out tonight – it's quiet, the houses are silent. The town is all lit up in stillness – you'll see – just how you like it."

Christmas lights pulled through my mind, but it wasn't.

"Okay," I said.

I rode up front with Teresa. "Pronounced with a small t," she said.

She was twenty. She was white-colored. She sat light, she felt like aluminum to me, with air in it.

"Did I ever tell you about my sister?" I asked her. Teresa drove the car with a big steering wheel in her small hands.

"Some, maybe once," she said.

"When she was a little girl, she skated all the time, all over town in the streets and on the sidewalks. She used to jump over things in her way. She lived on skates, she used to say. It's how she got around. She used to eat with them on her feet."

"Did she go to sleep in them, ever?"

"No. Well, maybe. She might have."

Teresa said, "Yeah. Look at the street, Carl. Emptied."

"Our mother had red hair, like sunburn, like if you had a new sunburn on your skin," I said. "Like a lobster color."

"Uh huh..." Teresa had a lonely mouth, and her head was soft.

"My mother was from England. Her mouth was English. She had broken-looking teeth."

"Everybody from there has that," she said.

"She skated everywhere. Over fire-hydrants, and junk. Over low fences. She was afraid of the dark... I am too," I said. "I don't have any place anymore to be in. My head hurts all the time."

"You're here, with me," said Teresa.

"She was skinny, and bright."

Teresa said "Uh, huh."

"I was out in the field tonight. I sat on the ground and felt how big it is." I continued. "I felt how BIG it really is. It's big, like a little girl's heart is."

"It is big," said Teresa.

"Think of the huge world drawn on coloring paper."

We drove on. Teresa was easy to see. I imagined how she would look from the back seat, her head, and maybe her face, partially lit in the mirror. I knew her for a couple of years.

I said quietly, to the cool window, "Shiny's hands, so warm and nice, on me, so small...so quiet how her fingers touched, each other -

"Cover me up," I said. I was drunk, I knew. I remembered it. "Cover my face with something - with your shirt... "

Teresa pulled over and covered me with her blouse, a dark, soft, sweatshirt, as best she could.

"Can you get under?" she said. "Can you get in?" She laughed, and she stopped.

I stayed in her chest for awhile. I thought of Shiny skating, again. I knew everything about her childhood. Almost twenty-five years, I thought, since I'd seen her face.

Teresa's chest was like a small Europe. I waited. I talked to her. We were together in one seat.

"Once, she had to jump over a dead horse," I said. "A horse that she knew. She said she cried. She cried like a girl. She had these fingers.... She said she went back and they were dragging the horse like it was stiff, dragging it with its legs sticking up, into a truck.

"Teresa, I like it in here," I told her. It's warm." She leaned against me, closer.

"It doesn't matter, any of that," she said. "It's all so still..."

"And scary," I said. I felt like a dead stick.

"Let's go," she said. I wanted to bury me and her under the lawn, together.

We drove. The cars rolled by us with other people in them talking about their lives.

"Once, all I had was a cut foot," I said. "It's all I had. I didn't have any friends, or a girlfriend, or a job, or a neat place to live.

Or any money, or any hope for any of that. But at night under my hot sheet – I slept on a slice of foam in a warehouse – it was rough. I felt my foot all night. It was something to have. It was all I had."

"Well, I'm glad you and that married woman are through," I heard Teresa say. "She was killing you."

I shook my head. "I don't talk about that." I said. "I don't want to."

Joey. I could never let go of her, but she had. It hadn't been too hard for her, married and safe. She had a nice life to ride around in and look out of. She never looked back. She touched me everywhere with her hands.

I called Teresa sometimes. I thought of her. "Hello," she'd say, in a voice, with cream in it. It was sweet, like a toy.

I said, 'Hi' to her. It sounded stupid. Her mouth was over there, across town. "I was thinking of you, and I wanted to talk to you. But now I have to go."

She said, "What was it about?"

"Nothing bad," I said. "I was just feeling good about you."

"Oh," she said.

I wanted to get inside her. She was so white and soft, like tennis balls. She was a girl.

If I asked her, said I wanted to love her, I'd be afraid she'd say no. I was also afraid she'd say yes.

"I'm too shy," I could have told Teresa on the phone, or anywhere. Her hands are so lightweight, they are floating, to hold in mine; to lay her down like a young couch, and pet her, so grave.

In her car she put my face under her shirt. The taste of her, in the dark there, as she sat by her own passenger, side window. I could almost not feel her touch when her hand was on my back. I got to be like a child.

I put off sleep, because I can't. I wake up early, to cough. My eyes are like two burnt holes in a blanket. I try not to, but

I crave a girl, Cokie, from the neighborhood, but she's only fourteen, "almost-sixteen," she says.

'I had to jump over a dead horse,' Shiny said. 'A friend of mine.'

I was scared of Teresa. I watched words twist in her mouth, like dirt. Her chest had been a child's shore. Teresa. I wanted her to make me love her, something, again; a dead horse with its legs like that, and dragged. I'd forgotten so many years, poured out.

Joey'd said: "You're either angry, or drunk."
I told her, "It'll get so windy out, we'll die. I'm afraid of little girls - their hearts; they remind me, of before, of when there was God" Joey looked like that, but she was a woman, a married person.

Grape juice stained Cokie's teeth. Her teeth were too big for her mouth. Her mouth — warm, and wet, and soft. And open.
Cokie said, "I dare you. To kiss my mouth." And she yelled it, in my house: "My mouth!" It was stained with purple color on her tongue and lips.
Shiny'd had those redcolors. When she held them, I thought they were like her mouth. She, and me, both watched them held by her thumb and first finger. It created a space, triangle and pointed, and her holding them like that and sitting, and being, were my favorite shapes, memorized.
Teresa was driving the car. I couldn't drive; there were figures in the road.
"It's this cold air I love," I told her. "It's clearing me up." I could make out Teresa's arm and her face, whitened by the dash light that flickered with age.

"An old car in a ditch, rusted, and ruined, or just parked, is to me more interesting than a city of buildings, or an airplane."

Teresa's little voice said something I couldn't hear. Maybe she said she liked planes. We were moving into nowhere.

"I'm scared of heights; I don't know how planes stay up. I mean, I do, sort of – cause there was this old guy once who came to my grade school, and he had all this stuff and gave an exhibit of how things worked, you know. I remember him up in the front of the room. He blew up a red balloon and let it go: it buzzed around the room, and he said, 'See, that's how a jet airplane works.' That stuck in my mind." I told Teresa, "It's the only thing I ever learned.

"Now that I think about it, about that guy, I bet he was a really blown old guy. Look how he made a living. I'd like to do that, go to kids' classes and show them how certain things work. Like drop things to show them about gravity, like a cannon ball, and a lighter, all the same. I could throw some books out the window."

"They'd like that," Teresa said. She reminded me of Cokie's childish face.

"And that balloon thing. Imagine doing that for a living. It'd be great. I'd drive to all the local schools, in all the towns around here. I'd have to drive alone to them. I could think, on the way, about anything I wanted to, and have a drink in the car, an old car, like a '54 Ford. I'm gonna do it. I'll call the schools tomorrow, and set it up. I'll show them about how animals live, desert ones, underwater strange ones. I'll draw on the board."

Teresa had nothing to do but drive. I reached over and touched her some while she drove. I stared at the road.

I felt myself going to the schools, doing the shows, a man doing 'Show and Tell' for children, and then I saw how it'd really be, me with a black bag of things to tell about, how it would end up with me out in the car, with a girl out there with me and I'd watch her mouth – while she talked about herself – and how she'd trust me. I kissed my sister. Then, the girl, and the balloons in the car, a cannon ball between us; her face would be bound to cry, and maybe me and her running, in a field – just to DO something, to live. I got quiet, I got down in it, and how it would always end up.

Teresa listened as she drove on. There were dirt fields outside, and miserable people in some of the places we passed – most of them, never as pretty as the grocery aisles at night, and the children.

We drove by a deserted prison, way back off the road.

"Everything I see..." I said, and I knew how small we were, the two of us, with our hands and faces... "– is so beautiful. The trees, the shapes, the shadows..." They were all so bright.

"Once, I leaned against that prison wall, and screamed."

* * *

"Kiss me," said Cokie, with her girl face, from her newer mouth; it was wet. It was like her, like only she could be, and it was so dear, and it was early tasting.

"No," I said at first, "I can't. I can't."

On her chest I saw the shape. She pulled off her yellow T-shirt. I had been holding my hand on her back, underneath it.

"I might as well take it off," she said. "You've got it all pulled up already, anyway. Here," she said. She handed it to me. It draped, loose, yellow in my hand.

"See?" she said. "Look."

She sat, small in the big chair. She held out her arms wide at me; she was herself, white and cool, small, and clean; the naked chest of a young girl, about to become big.

"Let me get you a towel," I said. "To cover you. I can't – do this." I felt like I was falling.

On her chest, as she held herself out to me, I saw the shape, like spilled liquid, bright, and alive, like the road-side figures in the night when they had been so distinct: they stuck out, and she had that shape, reddish like a broken bottle of wine.

"No!" I said. "How did you get here? How did I?"

"You asked me. You asked my mom."

"Yeah, but how? You don't understand. You – you're like a little puppet sitting in that big chair." And she laughed.

"I like to be here," she said.

"Put on your shirt." I held it out to her.

"No, you took it off. You put it back on me."

"You're too small," I said, "to be here like this." There were flowers outside in the dark. Seeing her naked in my chair, and so bold, made me drunk.

"I'm almost sixteen—"

"I know," I said. "I know that." I twisted my hands in her shirt. Something like a shovel was pushing me at her, in my chest, in my throat, in my body.

"Kiss my mouth again. I like it," she said. "Kiss me here." She put her fingers to her chest.

"No," I whispered, defeated. "I'll bundle you up into the car. You have to go home now."

"My arms," she said. "Kiss them, too." They were white painted sticks. I was falling from a great height. My heart pounded my ribs. She laid down on the floor and bent herself into a shape. I was terrified. She was snakelike. She raised her backside, and squirmed along the carpet. The shape was raised in places on her narrow back, and it twisted me. I thought of how my two fingers, with my palms on her back, reached around so my fingertips could touch her where she wanted me to. And I held her around her young, her pretty ribcage.

A fallen person so close to me.

Everything was so long ago, when I turned from the floor and saw Cokie's back as she ran out into the summer night, ran home either to tell, or lie awake all night in her bed, alone and wondering about things, and the smells that were new. I saw her face as they became new to her. She wore a red birth mark on her back. I'd seen something else on her chest, her chest like a sidewalk.

She had laughed at things that were easy, and hard, for me to say.

I would entertain a classroom with a balloon.

I could think about her, because I was older, but would she dare?

I saw her, then, through the screen-door shut behind her. She ran. I thought of her going home, like a cripple, to her own front door, her face crippled too, Cokie, changed, different now, torn into a new shape by me.

* * *

"What was the orange liquid you fed her?"

"Purple," I told her Mother.

"Purple," said her Dad. He was trying to stand up strong. He wanted to crease his eyes, and lay down and cry at what he thought, but he couldn't.

"Yeah, purple," he said. "What was that you gave her? Her mouth had it all over her."

"Nothing," I said. "Grape drink is all."

The girl, Cokie, going out into her life on crutches made by her and me, together, her mother watching her from the front door each time she leaves. Then, she turns and retreats back into her empty, daughterless house-place.

* * *

Teresa curved the wheel around a long, slow curve.

"Why don't you hit something," I said. "Hit another car, Teresa, going fast."

If we hit another car, and got hit, too, from behind and from the side, we would turn in circles, we would spin. It would throw us, shake us from the dream, take us out of our mind-cloth, our thoughts, and our prisons. We would become abandoned prisons.

"Hit something! Please! I want to go some place else."

"Yeah, well, I don't know," said Teresa. "I don't know how to do that," she said. So we rode on in the grand. It was a great darkness that came at us.

"I was always scared to have a good time," I said. "So I turned to weird time in the dark."

There had been Joey, the married girl I loved. She told me not to cry. I was left with a crippled child I made.

"I love a small town —" I said.

I grabbed at Teresa's mouth. "I can just go out, and wander, and stumble out in the grass, and the corn in the fields in the dirt. I could fall down, and in the morning just get up and walk home. Or if a farmer guy found me, or a lone dog, or two, it'd be okay. I don't care. I can just put my collar up against the cold. I could die."

I whispered to Teresa, "I don't want Jesus, or Mary, to hear me. But, I just don't care anymore," I said. "I just don't."

"Yeah. But I want you to be safe."

I heard myself thinking: 'Joey, don't go. Please, I'm scared of it, of all the empty time without you, before you, and after. What will I do when I see your house? Don't go...' but it was an old echo by then, an old house fallen down with time where people used to live. Her hair was still all over my house on the floor. She told me goodbye out at a park. I watched her leave, and I stayed there for a long time. I couldn't leave. I found the Kleenex she left on the ground.

"Your crazy mouth," Teresa said. Mine was stained with purple.

Shiny gone, Joey, gone. And Cokie's chest, and the shape, Mom, your shape out on the rug.

When Joey left she ripped another shape into being. It was a shape like a torn page, her gone-shape, jagged into my sight. It was like bad glasses on.

"Teresa," I told her. "Teresa is my light."

"You tasted me," she said, "like I was candy."

* * *

Cokie writhed on the floor, a picture. She curved herself, till she bled juices; she became a pushing at me. Her lips were purple and shaking.

I got down on my knees to see her close, to feel her new heat.

I kissed her, her side-chest wall, soft, then over, sucking hard.

I reached with my face. I kissed at her mouth like gold. I ate there at her. I drank her mouth. I knew her. I tasted her; I loved, I kissed her red liquid lips. Cokie, how could your chest, flat, and sweetened, have that shape, like the one from my mother's head that was shot, by herself, that was bled into the shape, as it escaped – of a terrible lake?

* * *

"Everything is a horrible shape," I said.

"Close your eyes," said Teresa. "Just take it easy. Let's get past all this."

My mother's hand held the gun that shot a hole in her head that let her bleed a shape, a shape that was childless, and red, into the white rug she fell down on. She fell down.

"Why know anything?" I asked her. "Why do anything at all?" I said.

"To kiss me some more –" she said. "That's why." She talked sideways to me. She turned to me while she drove a car.

"No," I said.

Me and Shiny, me and shiny apalaris. She hopped, she laughed, she jumped in her little dress - in her legs, in her blood.

I thought I saw myself out the window; it rained before, on my shack, alone.

"All you have to do is open your mouth and let me in," she said. "Just like before –"

She leaned over when the car was quiet; it sat heavy on the roadside.

She made me, I laid against her, and while at first I enjoyed the soft, and she held my head like a child – she changed.

From her angel, into a lake of blood.

"I can't stand it!" I said. My voice came from outside me, from the past. "I don't want it to be this way!"

"Let me out. I have to stand up on the ground, on the ground at some place." Shiny always saw what I was.

I got outside the car. Teresa got out too.

She said, "I know you, how it is. It's quiet out here, isn't it?"

I said, "Yes." It was. We were quiet; things buzzed.

I looked at her.

"I liked it," I said. "No one knows, though." My eyes burned. "I miss people. I'm afraid I'll die soon. I know I will. That young girl I know – she's so good. But she's no substitute. I'll miss you, too, soon."

Teresa caught my wrist. The car did a slow turn by itself when she'd jumped out after me. Jumped-out, with a ghost in the back. She wore pants, they were day-blue, and I looked back and saw that color when she ran across, in front of her headlights.

"Let me go," I said. "Let me out here."

"No," she said, "No! What have you been talking about? What do you think you did? Tell me! Now!"

"No – what she did –"

"Who, your mother? Or Joey? Or some little girl – was she your sister? Tell me!"

We were out in the dirt. Teresa shone, throwing her whiteness on me, her youngness. I was there, evil. "I used to be like you," I said. "And like a girl, too. That's why I like you, and like to kiss you."

"You act like you don't even know who I am sometimes."

"I forget. I forget almost everything. Never the shapes though – I can see them. Everywhere I look, always, like I wear glasses that have a stain on them. The shapes, from women. One I was born in, and the other I was born near – she's lost. One I was born to meet. It's funny, they're gone but they left their shapes on me – actually on my eyes. The only women I really liked.

"Where are we?" I asked her. I kept waking up again, and again...

Teresa held herself, above me. "Where?" she asked. "We're just after being in the grocery store. We're outside, here in the dark, Carl. Just look—"

"Why do you go there all the time?" she said. "I always see you there late at night."

"You know why. Same reason you go there. To feel safe. To see the colors..." I felt my face breaking.

I felt one main thing – a desire to be let go of, to be let to fall, all the way. To be away from the weight: what a child had been, and done, twice to me. Now, Teresa, dirt-sexual, was here. She offered herself to me, like a pretty colored plate to lick clean. It wasn't her chest, or her heart; she was an entire place to live in, how she knew herself, the feminine thing she carried with her.

There were angels near our world. They cared for Shiny now.

"Girl," I said. "Don't watch my mouth, if I tell you —"

"Okay," she said.

"It's broken," I said.

"What is?" and she looked at me.

"My voice. My telling voice, the truth..."

She laid her hand on my arm.

"Don't," I said. "I'm scared, of everything."

"Not me?"

"Yeah —"

"I could help you; I came for you," she said.

"No, I'd hurt you. I'd want to --"

"Carl – tell me what you see. About the shapes, and the other thing."

"When I was a kid, we took someone, we made her come with us, and we covered her. We covered her up in the ground."

"With what?"

"We put her under the ground – not deep, but just to show her, I guess, what we were. Boys. I didn't want to. Then we pulled her out."

"Tell me what you did. It's okay. It won't hurt me. It was a long time ago, Carl."

"We didn't do that much. We were young – but not that young. I don't know."

"What?" And from Teresa's throat came the girl, the same sound, the sound we feared, and loved, and wanted, and didn't understand, and hurt.

"We, they, bled on her. We cut ourselves, blood-brothers, and then they held her and bled it all over her."

"On her face?"

I looked at Teresa's mouth, and her brain. "Yeah. And, she had dirt all over her, and her clothes got torn, and then, I watched, I got away without them noticing – they all kissed her. She got where she didn't seem to care that much. They did other stuff to her, too, on her."

I saw Teresa mixing it all up on her face. It wasn't pretty; it was what we had been, together, even her, the girl, Shiny. And Teresa knew, like the girl had: even though I tried to hide from her, that I hadn't been able to keep away. The girl's hands were enough to make me, draw me in. They twisted together in front of her face. She touched her face with her fingers.

Teresa said, "I chased you out here in the dark. You've been my friend." The car lights were still on, shining on the road, lighting it. "I followed you into this weird place."

"Yeah – I know. I could be gone in a minute, it's happening so fast. I'm dying – my reasons not to are running away from me – I'm scared to death."

I saw her face try to hold me. I felt mine wanting to come apart. I saw the shape on her. "Oh, God! I can't stand it! I want to see you, but I can't look at you."

That had been the whole thing: the not-looking.

"My mother said to me, she said, and I'll never forget it, 'I saw you, Carl, why were you standing and staring when I saw you. What's wrong?' I was scared of her face, to see me, when she knew, when she found out what we had done. To her daughter."

"That was a long time ago," said Teresa. There was a little light shining down there, at the road.

"What do you mean, long ago? It's now! It's not – there's no long ago. That's stupid. There's no yesterday. It's happening now! It's all taking place right now, forever." Teresa looked at me, and she knew. "She's doing it, now, don't you understand?"

She gaped on her young face. She saw some of the time stacked up, that made things look old, the weight, the straining.

"I don't understand you at all," she said.

"A lot of times I look at those buildings, those old buildings downtown. They look so odd, so unreal; I could run and put my hand through them. There's no one on the streets but me late at night. I saw you going by the other night. I was at the end of an alley. You were driving – you were coasting.

Teresa, she was like someone's sister. Her blonde hair blew into her face. She let it be there that way. Then it blew away.

"That night, it was last night – I was watching a cat, a yellow one going into the alley, the alley below the windows. I love to be alone and just see something like that. It disappeared in the dark."

We were quiet.

Like a picture it came on again. "It just won't let me be," I said. "Teresa! She saw my face. And then I saw hers!"

"Who? My God! You scared me," she said.

"Her. She knew what I did – to my sister, to my own sister. To Shiny. So, I killed her. I pulled the trigger. I tried to sneak up on her, so she would never have to see me, to look like that at me, after she knew. Once you know, then that's it, you have to always know. And she turned her head, and in a second, in one, long moment that lasts still until now, she saw.

"I told myself she didn't, she never saw me after she knew, but I know the difference a lie can make. A young lie, old now— and then that shape she made in me, it all became one thing..."

"What are you saying?"

"She turned, I shot her in the head, and she fell down and she bled to death lying down on the carpet in the dinning room, and me and Shiny watched her do that....I shot and killed my poor mom."

The breeze made noise as it turned in Teresa's hair.

"I adore you," she said, "cause you're on the dot, the dotted line, you're in that special place, before something happens – like death, or something big. I've seen it all around you. You're crowding something weird like no one I ever saw."

Adore, adore, adore, she danced around our house once upon her time...

"I wish," I told her, "I wish you knew, and could be with me, so with me that you were me. But you aren't. You never will be." I wanted her to cover me, so I could stop. Cover me with a long red coat, a wool, thick, bright red coat, with bright buttons on it, but out in the dark, always. I asked her to.

"I know you never killed anybody," she said. "You never did anything, it's only wishes, sick twisted memories of nothing."

* * *

The yellow cat; it ran. It followed a blacker cat. "Kitty," I said. They leaked heat in them.

Cover me with a red coat.

Why are there cats and dogs? Why are they here? I thought. Shiny knew. I walked in the alleys all over town. I expected things to run out at my feet, but they never did. Just shadows, of old spoken words…

"I want to be a man, and I'm not," I told the cats. I followed the shadows, "but only for a little while," I said. "I'm only here for a little while."

* * *

"Nothing but wishes, Carl."

"Take me back to the square," I said. I motioned, wide armed at her. I gestured for myself, alone, a gentle thing, like a young girl could make, maybe at the sky, at someone's eyes, only for myself.

"Take me back where you picked me up. Where I can see things stay the same. To the cemetery," I mumbled. I didn't want her to hear me anymore.

Teresa had a footlocker full of dolls. I'd seen them, touched them, their faces and pretty. They all had names.

"The less a place it is, the better."

"What?" she said. She had a slanted face.

"Nothing," I said. "Take me back."

In the car, in the pieces, we flew through the sound of the quiet night. I had held her. She had been a play-pretty for me. The pipes were blowing off the bottom of the car.

"No one cares," Teresa said to me, "if there ever was a girl like that, a sister. Just you. She's all grown up by now, and working somewhere, or dead. She doesn't care. And if it is true, she probably looks back on it as a fun-thing, something sort of wild. If she was touched, or messed with, or whatever it was. She's just like the rest of us now, one-time special."

I saw something outside on the street – some people, three purple pictures. Three people standing out under a restaurant light, the only late night place in town. I was part of the old age, the world that was dying. Whatever was coming, I didn't want to forget, forget the games I played as a boy, with my father, and the night, and the way certain light was as it played along the face of a trusting, sleeping girl.

The Pizza sign, it was a cry, a rip in the heart of town. I wanted to walk along the streets, alone, in cherished loneliness. There, the green, tall, huge building where nothing ever moved. Who were the three, in a purple sign-light? People, who must have known something. Like dogs, they were here.

We passed by the corner where Joey said her last words to me, in her hushed, husky, cry-voice. "Don't," became her favorite word to me, and then, "I-have-to-go." I whistled after her when she ran away down the hill. I whistle there always to get safely past after midnight from her ghost.

Then, past the old high school, I thought of an empty young girl, laid down, expecting better, and seeing six boys above her, some of them laughing, she being drawn to the one that wasn't, and then it being still, and rapid, and them getting all over her – and her face, where she lived from, from where she saw – her baby face, raped, and her mother turning her head too soon to let me know that she knew - that she knew what I was.

I told myself in between the garbage cans in the black alleyway where the cats lived, "Don't be, Time. Don't be, don't... anymore."

"Let me off in the dark.," I said.

"Carl..."

We drove. It was over. All the words had disappeared.

She pulled over. "Well, do you have to get out now?" she said.

"Yeah." As it got still, we breathed again the cool air from the town.

"Thanks for the ride," I said. "Teresa." So she smiled.

"Seeya at the grocery store," she said.

"No. You won't."

"Then I'll miss you," she said. "I will."

She shot off. She was dragging her feet under the little car.

So what? I thought. So what? I was looking for someone to dig me a fresh hole I could lay down in. Lay me down on my back, my hands over my heart. Cover me up, like we did to her; cover me with a red coat all my own.

CHAPTER 5

I walked back the few blocks over to the restaurant, where there would be light for awhile. Teresa, a woman-girl, I thought, lost light and grease. I watched the sidewalk as I walked it, and soon saw a purple light growing on it.

I went in and took a seat, a secret seat along the side. There were cactuses in pots there. There was a waitress; she was so tired. She sat. She got up to bring me a drink to hold with my hand. Her hair fell.

When I looked up again, there were three women who came into the place. One – she was smaller than the other two. There was something about her, immediately seen, something wrong. Before they got to their booth – and the dirt in the fields outside being there made it okay for them to walk slowly, to hold up this person, and okay for the one to let go before she sat down: her hands curled up, her fingers almost to her wrists. Her knees pressed together in her blue jeans. Her feet turned inward. Her face – it touched me – was innocent ecstasy, a blood-daughter to Christ, Jesus bending down and twisting to touch that face – her, an epileptic in my night. Her eyes rolled up, and I thought: who is this? Was there a blood taste in her mouth too, like mine had?

This girl, she calmed down immediately. Then, she jerked, wild and holy. In her small, lighted place to be, she flipped about, by herself on one side of the table. Her hair was cut shortish, making her round eyes look bigger, cut short so it couldn't fly too much. She made scary faces, then quickly changed back to her other beauty. Her, like a little horse, new, and jumping itself around in its grass field, then stopping to look at you in the face. I wrapped myself up in the chills I felt, and in the embarrassment I had over the last twenty years before seeing this wonderful girl.

Maybe she was playing; maybe I could know her.

She turned her thin neck; she turned her face towards me. She saw me sitting there. My face must have looked like white paper, suspended, above dark clothes, sitting in the darkness. Her eyes looked at me, absorbing, then there was a short, easy, half-smile. I flinched. It caught up with me.

I got up. I went into the restroom and barely got the door closed behind me when it broke from me. The years I had in there came out, in the face of this simple smile, that carried with it Shiny's lost face to see, even Joey's: how could it happen to us?

This girl with her smile was out there.

I felt her, how she sat on the seat of the booth. I felt I was of her. I bent over the sink, saw its streaked whiteness. I washed my face in the dripping cold

* * *

The girl in the booth, she let me watch her.

She knew it was me who watched. She knew we were in the same water. I sat and stared at her. She turned fully at me now. She mouthed silent, shaped words across the space of the room: "Don't stare." She smiled, again, wide, her teeth all lined up even this time.

Her legs bucked suddenly up against the underside of the tabletop. A glass knocked over and ran. They laughed about it. I worried there would be a single, naked nail sticking down that would go into her thigh. I felt under my own table for the nail, but it was smooth – then there, there was one.

Feeling under the table, crouched back, I was a coward, remembering her as in a bright morning. I knew who this girl was. She'd been in there, in-between my breaths, all along.

When she got up to leave, she walked better, her mouth went open half way, her head went back some. She was carving out a space for me not to forget her ecstatic gestures in. She leveled her eyes at me. She shot out a secret to me. The brightest light couldn't have made her blink.

I felt my hand up at my mouth, touching. She leaned slightly on one of the women. She saw me from her watery heart.

I went over to where she had been, and put my hand where hers had rested. I held it there where it was warm. I kept it there. I saw myself from outside the place, and as very small. I saw myself pick up something from the table and throw it as hard as I could, through the front, plate glass window that had a painted sign all on it.

CHAPTER 6

I came back to myself, here, put into jail.

That strange girl that I saw: I pictured her face on my jail window, sort of lit up there, like a gift. She wouldn't go away. She could seep through the thick fingered glass window.

She would be somewhere, sleeping at night, her hands curled, pretending, or really being that way. She filled the whole town with her shapes, small, and huge, writhed, and charmed-full.

She might have to share a bed; she'd be well over on her side, favorite side, maybe with her own colored sheet, two colors on one bed, with some sister, or brother, or uncle. Her mouth would hold itself, quietly her own, jumping about in her sleep time.

CHAPTER 7

A sign on the judge's tall desk said not to lean there on it. I never would've.

"I might be guilty," I said, "but I don't want to be...

"What will I do with my house, and my things?" I asked, and I saw: What about the strings? The strings on the children who crawl nearby that are the different colors moving around my house – they're the orbits, and my gray house is a shrine to the memory of how it once was.

They crawl near it and around it to make a galaxy.

"What about all the children I live near?" I said.

"If you are sentenced to incarceration that will be attended to. There are procedures," he said, and it trailed away. I was in a smoke filled room of old boards.

A female lawyer came in early to talk to me. She looked like a cousin I saw only one time. I tried to tell her what I did and why: "I was on six months probation. Because her husband, he hurt Joey. He probably raped her. I went to their house, and I saw it, through the window, and I blew up. It was all so neat, and orderly there. I hated it. I went over to their house, where maybe I shouldn't have. I loved her..."

"But that was before," she said. "What about last night?"

"I don't really know," I told her. I didn't. "I remember, I felt good, and bad, and someone threw something. It was me, I guess –"

"Yes," she said.

And she read me my rights.

"Why would you use anything against me?" I asked her. "Aren't you my lawyer? I need to talk about this —"

"No," she said. "I'm the prosecuting attorney." I saw myself eating many plates of stormy, darkened, brown French toast. Please, there's too much syrup, or not enough. I don't even smoke. I might as well live here.

Six months didn't sound too long, since I knew I wouldn't make it anyway. I destroyed property. It made me sad at Joey's house, and last night, not so sad, but something.

I wouldn't have leaned in against the desk either way.

Smoke set in, and as the jailer and I walked two short blocks back to the jail, I heard him say: "...there are these maps, and some special charts of lakes showing their shapes and sizes, their depths and locations," and he stepped in such a way that I skipped to fall into place with him. My father showed me that once with Shiny when she was a baby. He held her up, off the ground.

'And there are all these shapes between everything. Sometimes that's all I see, not any things, like houses or trees or boats, whatever is there, but the shapes between them all; it's the world in between everything. The one we see but don't see. It's hard to use it other than to feel it; there's mathematics to it, calculating the size of no-shapes, and ...'

I found myself asleep, again, sometimes curled, sometimes straight, waking once in awhile into a cleared field. It was best when I slept, getting to be all alone. Were there really maps of strange lakes, and of the shapes of that other world? Did he say those words to me? In the day I couldn't see through, but at night I entered in there, into that world, sometimes.

I washed floors. I paid close attention to each clean tile, the lines that made it square. It wasn't real tile, it was rusty

colored, one foot each. It was in the lines where the dirt collected. I remembered then. It was from watching my hands on
the mop handle, worn, something to hold onto. It was shined
up from so many different hands. It was Shiny come back to
my memory:

One time our family went on a car trip, for ninety miles –
we went all the time to see my father's aunt. She had a Boston
terrier, a little black and white dog with a pig-like, push face.
On the way, I was asleep for part of what happened, for what
Shiny did.

We had a station wagon, it was old, reddish looking, and
rusted along the crack where the back laid down. We liked to
fold it up and sit in the way back. We could watch out at the
road running behind us, in a turn-around seat. There was a
man who fell in behind our car.

"He was following us," Shiny told me, "and waving a lot.
Every minute he could wave at me he did. Then he put his
hand out the window to point at me and wave some more, and
later he put his face out and stuck it out at me. I could feel him
getting near me. I kept watching, too. It made me feel really
uncomfortable. He got uncomfortable too, and tried to look
away, to look down, but he couldn't, cause he was driving. He
pretended to play with the radio and in the glove compart-
ment, but he stayed driving pretty close. He could've slowed
down, or turned off, but he didn't.

"Then he started again – you were asleep. I saw your mouth
sleeping open. You were funny. You were so tired from watching
TV up late, I remember. The guy started waving a lot and then
he was trying to talk to me with his hands and move his mouth
really big so I could read it. He was making big ideas with his
hands for me to read, to see. He pounded on the car and inside,
and even on his head. He was mad at somebody, at himself it
looked like mainly – for doing something. It was stuff about
his heart, his feelings, I could tell. He was telling me he had a
problem with his heart.

"Dad saw him in the rear-view mirror, and told me to stop it. I said I was just watching a crazy guy, and he said to stop it – to turn around or lay down – or to come up front. So I did. I left you back there."

I woke up when the man drove alongside and honked and yelled out his car window at us.

"The little girl," he yelled. "I tried to tell her – that I can't keep living – not like this." He yelled this from the opposite lane, riding even.

"See – my wife..." and he told a short story about how his wife... And my Dad motioned to him and we all pulled over. Dad liked the man. They got out cigarettes, and smoked, and talked. They walked down the highway shoulder. The man still kept turning and waving over at Shiny the whole time. Once he seemed to cry; he leaned in against my Dad's shoulder. He still held a short, white, smoking cigarette in his hand, hanging down. We were outside with cars going by fast, in colors that blurred.

My mother's hair looked so clear and clean, and bright, out in the air that day. It looked red, but it was mainly brown. It was the sunshine out there on the highway, stopped in the country between two cities that did it. Her fingers looked extra white. They held each other and touched, tucking her hair into her collar, away from her face. I liked it best when it hung into her face, carving it different each time.

She was nervous; she bit the inside of her mouth. She didn't say much then, but did a few short laughs and quick snorts that would go away as fast as they came out, so fast it was like they never happened. Everything was like that as soon as it was over.

She appeared as thin as the air; she looked like a bad girl. Her life was like a cigarette smoking down.

The man shook hands with me, and Shiny. He was short and looked like he'd smoked cigarettes his whole life. His skin had a canned, and tired, yellow-brown look. He moved quick though, and animated. He shook hands a long time with Shiny. He followed us all the way to North Jackson. We left him behind in the traffic of the city. It looked big to me when we were in it. Then he faded in with the others.

He was like a package of cigarettes, the short kind, and like that quick smell, right when the pack is opened by the little pull string.

Shiny said he made a whole story with his hands, all full of ideas and feelings, and filled up the front seat of his car and the back seat of ours with his life. "It was too big for his insides to hold," she said. "His face got on mine some, too close."

He was a little wind-up guy that couldn't stop until he died. His little arm pumped. I saw his muscles, tanned, under the old, dark, burned hair on his forearms.

"I knew exactly how he felt," she told me. "Sick. And with sharp pains in him. He was really, really uncomfortable, because he had to look away from everyone all the time. When he spit, I know he felt weird about that, too, but he couldn't help it, it was a habit. He was a mess."

I was like that man now. He was dead probably. I held onto the mop; I leaned on it. I could see Shiny by the roadside. A man, trying to tell his problems to a little girl, with sign language. In the years ahead he probably blew up in himself. He was wild, like rubble, like some ruins in a gray colored city. Dad told him when Shiny's birthday was.

* * *

Leaning on my mop, I could see the cage out to the side of the building where we could go, the prisoners, to get fresh air, and light. I had that slit window. The others did, too. They went outside and sat in the cage. There were only two others. And they were brothers, due to get out any day. They had a similar look, slant mouthed. They were fear-colored.

I didn't want to go out there. You had to wear a red jump-suit, so if you got through the cage, through a closed cyclone fence, and ran, it'd be easy to see you. Then they could kill you.

I stayed in my cell. Usually I thought of nothing. Sometimes, of Shiny, was all. I watched my hands, amazed sometimes that I was connected even at all to them, or to anything. I watched them as they touched places, held my things, and touched other people. I only touched the jailer once or twice, to get his attention. He wore a gray shirt that I touched with my hand, lightly.

I touched myself some. And I held my palms upwards, flat on my thighs. I could only do it for short times.

One day, the brothers were gone. Their thick and their slurred words and their looks at me were gone. And me, like a stick in a shadow, I flinched.

I went outside for an hour, in the cage. I saw the outside world through the fence, through the little sideways squares. Shiny always made things get little. I sat on the cool concrete floor, in a red jumpsuit.

Shiny made the world little by putting her fingers together and looking through them at people. They'd fit into that tiny place, or she'd curl her hand and look through it like a telescope to make a big thing look small. Shiny's hand, like a telescope.

The man who pulled our car over and smoked, and maybe cried, and laughed too fast - she did that to him.

"This is Elizabeth, our daughter," my Dad said. "Some-times we call her Shiny."

"I can see that," he said, with smoke in his mouth. "I could see that from forty feet away." He put his hand out to touch her near her shoulder, where her hair was just above. She had on a small, light-blue blouse. I could still see the folds in it, the wrinkles. It came to just an inch above the waist of her brown pants.

It came out at me now, ferociously — that she had really been. She was under that shirt, under that day, that place, that time. I squeezed myself inside deeper. I protected her there, in that memory place. He touched Shiny.

"Hi," she said. She put up two fingers and peeked through them at him, so he'd fit, like a tiny man. His face was large, and it seemed as if he didn't like it much. He looked away, and down. He had to push into a life like hers, or stay feeling sad.

I drummed on my knee with a pen. I had some paper, to pretend to write on. I needed something, out there, so exposed. I couldn't sit there alone. There was an ice cream place almost next door. There was a fence all around me, even the top was fenced in. I could see cars going slowly by the front part of the police station. The cage was hooked on to the low, one level building, a yellow-brick place. The cage sat in a parking lot, next to the ice-cream place, where children were.

CHAPTER 8

Shiny rode a little mechanical horse named Sandy, at the grocery store near where we lived. I watched her from the car, or at a safe distance. I stood on the dark cement, always too aware of being me.

"Carl, you ride, too," she said. "With me. Please. I don't want to ride it alone." I got over and sat behind her. It shook us for five minutes. I hated it. I buried my face in Shiny's back. I felt the future. I knew we'd be apart and alone. I squeezed her closer. She didn't mind. She was dear. I could taste her neck, where her hair just reached to. My mom saw us from the store window. Her make-up was on wrong. She looked like a sad, slanted, clown mom. She didn't smile. She held a bag of groceries, over and over, and never with any peace. I held to Shiny as hard as I could. She made a little noise.

* * *

I sat, and watched the sky in its small blue pieces, saw some birds, and watched the cars. The children were in their ice cream. I saw some of them walking. They stepped short steps. They were like the abandoned colors near my little house. Maybe I would've been dead by this day, if not here.

I lay down in my cell. I didn't speak for days. I reviewed the darkness. I got lost in all the years in between. I remembered my hand on someone's' shoulder. It was on Cokie's. She was a girl, not my sister.

I had her over once in awhile. She limped. She kissed. She lost all ability of being her certain age. I tasted her lips and her tongue, and her skin. Her skinniness, her life, its heart and its pulsing were a great child.

Sometimes she sat, and watched me, and watched the room, and never spoke. She pressed my palm to her flat chest. She bit my hand. She held it, cupped between her legs. She wore blue jeans. She touched my face, and she said my name.

"I like your hair," she said. "And your face. You're handsome," she said. "You make me cry." We were well beyond the world, sitting there in our own. Her mother, young once, before Cokie, was a pile of ruins. She never noticed how her daughter became sorry, withdrawn, confused, and a girl of imagined lovemaking, a faint idea: 'it's just a faint idea, sweet Cokie, what we do is an approximation…' 'Approximation?' 'Yeah. Imagined oneness, you and I…' at only fourteen. 'But I love you…' 'yes, yes, thanking you,' I told her upturned face, using an expression of my disappeared sister-love.

Now, as I watched from my cage – and I knew I belonged here – Cokie turned fifteen.

Lover, of a kind, in a house with many apologies. There were old notes here, older than Coke's very new-appearing breasts. Notes pinned to the wall unread for a year. Lover, of the kind, not pushed open, just held, half-naked and pure, warm and cool skin, and wet; Cokie, named that way cause she wouldn't drink much else, even as a baby, her milk snuck in a Coke bottle. All of us with nicknames, a child with a Coke bottle for a name, and some old man.

"It wouldn't be hard to tell you lies," I said. "Cokie, do you understand us, what we are, and do? That it's lonely, and thin? But lovely?"

"You called us approx-i-ma-shun…"

"I did, and it is, it can't be more than that, don't you see?"

"But it's more, it's all I have. I have a heart you know. It's all I really am."

She pursed her lips and sailed me a kiss from the littered floor where she sat.

Cokie would have real breasts now, the line between girl and woman, drawn. There would be Coca Cola from them. I saw that dark, fizzy liquid going into my mouth. I tasted it, sitting in the jail, semi-dark. Her babies would suck the Coke out of her body. She wouldn't grow into much more than a child because of it though, so maybe she'd always be that little way.

She visited me many times; they were like wild, bright flowers, her presence. I saw her on a swing-set one day, at her school. Her legs were white, and she had her socks and shoes on. She wore a sweater on top. She waved one hand at me, holding on.

One day she'd be older, then really old, with people maybe honking horns at her for being so old and driving so slow, maybe her even having a heart attack in the car, slowing down permanently. But, it was no real excuse. She was a phantom that disappeared one afternoon.

She was the youngest thing ever in my house, younger even than some of the magazines I had.

CHAPTER 9

The light was bright on my face, where there had been nothing before.

"Hey, Apalaris. It's breakfast. What kind of name is that, anyway?"

Eating time. Work time. Mop handle, then the cage. And more waiting. Maybe Cokie will show her face through the fence today. I hadn't seen her in months. She would be bigger one day. I'd be the same. I'd lean on a stick somewhere and my eyes would carry the little picture of her as a child. 'I never hurt her. I never hurt anyone,' I told me. 'Never.'

"Nothing's real," I said.

"What'd you say?" The jailer looked in at me. He held my breakfast tray.

"I said, how can anything be real if it's always disappearing? Like now," I said, and paused. "See. Gone. Where? Everything is always here and then gone. It bothers me."

"Here today, gone tomorrow," he said. "Time stops for no one, right?"

"Wrong," I said. I talked to his shadow.

He walked on by. I thought how it'd be if everything did stand still.

Later, I told him, "I got lost in my cell." I crawled in the hedge row.

"Yeah, I bet you did," he said. He turned a magazine page. "I bet you did."

Then, I liked him.

"Hey, jailer!"

"Yeah – what?"

"Hey, this is the most recent moment in the history of the universe."

* * *

I sat up much of each night. I propped my head up and looked at the light through the bars. I turned around and stared at the bare wall, with nothing to see. I was alone. There was no one, no one to call. I called information a few times, before.

"Shiny Apalaris," I asked. I called different cities. There never was anyone with that name.

"'Shiny Cleaners', is all I have," I heard.

"No, no, that's not it." I was afraid to ask for her real name, right, even if I knew it.

I lay on my back, on the cot over wire slats.

Shiny and I had slept together in my bed when I was a boy. Her face looked close up to mine. She dug into my side, and her face got under my arm.

It reminded me: Joey, later, was a shine. Her two lips; I only saw a cigarette hanging there once. I saw the side of her face that way, in a car. She rode the passenger seat, and I saw her, as she must've looked without me.

When I took her away – *kidnapped*, they said - she got a red face. She yelled, she spit, and she cried. I cuffed her to a tree, her arms held around it. It was like handcuffing my childhood there, to stop and look at it. It would never be mine again.

"I have to stop it all, for a minute," I told her. "No one knows we're here. We hardly even do." She watched me, her head shifting to either side of the tree to see me. She had her arms around it, and she faced it.

She said she hoped no one could see her, like that.

She wore a short, soft skirt, and a little shirt. I would've pinned a piece of bright colored tin there on it, if I had some. There would be slight bends in it, in the color.

She had shoes on before; they were gone. One was in the car on the floor. I unbuttoned her shirt. Her arms were beautiful in the silver bracelets. I took off her skirt.

I told her, "I know, Joey, you're the kind of girl who cries if you handcuff them." And she did. I kissed her mouth. It was wet. She kissed me back. I tasted her tears that came down. We kissed each other more than anything else, sometimes for hours. It was like a career. I ate her body, like a cake, at her tree. She knelt. She leaned against it.

We were at our cross, I thought then. Then I saw the whites of her eyes, in the dark. I took her home. Then I was in the jail, the first time here. The charges got dropped because she told them that she liked it.

One time we were outside sitting, and lying down on a quilt. It was cool out in the pines. We were just near pine trees. We heard something, from under the ground. It was a song. We went over and listened to it. It sounded very muffled, and we looked at each other. When we dug it up, it was a yellow radio someone had buried there, with batteries making it play.

Joey was hurt, often. Her husband did it to her. She got damaged. I didn't have to hear her say it. And I didn't, I never heard her voice again.

One time, before that, I said to her a word, "date-rape" and she spit. She spit everywhere, at me, on the floor, in the air, crazy with it.

"That's so stupid! Those words," she yelled, "are so fucking stupid. What about date-kill?" she said. "Would that be okay...I mean, as long as it was on a date? You fucker. You're probably a rapist too."

She read me an article in a Chinese restaurant. There were no Chinese people near there, where all the walls were paneled thin.

"Where have you been?" she asked. "No one sees you, ever."

"Nowhere," I said. "Home." Where Cokie limped.

The article was about a boy who had been missing for two months. She showed me the article, and the boy's picture. "I know him," I said. "I've seen him, walking around. I remember him cause of his hair."

"That's how his mother recognized him – by his jeans, and his hair."

Joey cried. She stood, and cried, in the small restaurant where the ceiling was too low, and paper-looking. She stood and cried.

She said through it, "He just went out and lay down in a cornfield and died... See?" And she poked at the paper. "See, it says he died of natural causes – he was found after being there for two months. Natural causes!" she cried. "He was only sixteen. He went out and lay down and died.

"Why was he so sad? Why was he so depressed, to do that? Think how a mother would feel?" She clenched up her fists and hit her chest, and her body. She wanted to break things apart, but she couldn't.

"Think how a child would feel," she said in the car, her blue car, going home.

* * *

I went over to Joey's, that last time, where her husband, the abuser, lived. He was on top of her; her, who I always loved.

I saw Joey. She didn't want me to. I saw her hitting, I saw her scream, I saw that dead boy out there, sad. So I smashed it all up. I saw her husband's stupid electric guitar. The way it was leaned, neatly, on his amplifier did it. That caused it. I broke it in half. I hit it over and over. He never said a word, but moved off into a dark corner.

He let Joey up, and she ran, with a hand up at her mouth. She held her shirt. I watched her go, where the stairs turned up, where the plaster came off the wall. Where I had known her. Her mouth always looked wet. Her running up the stairs inspired me.

I threw down the amplifier. It bounced off the hard wooden floor. I watched it. I picked it up and threw it at the window. It smashed through, and fell to the ground below. I wanted it to be me. So I threw a brown chair into the other window. It got stuck, busted through, halfway. There was a shape broke in the window. It held itself out to me. It had a mocking, but understanding shape to it. I looked at it, its sharp edges, the chair caught there. It made me wince. I almost reached out to it.

For the love, and that window, for what I did at Joey's house, I was in a jail now, over someone new, a girl I saw, making her own unique shapes in space that surrounded her.

Joey never pressed charges, but her husband did. I couldn't save her, or anyone. But in her neverness, her agedness, and loss, in that boy's laying down out there, and the smashed face of a mocking window, dear Cokie always in the backseat of where I am, and another, strange, quirky girl, all connected at a Holy place – that was the place where I would find Shiny.

* * *

When I was young, still a kid, the year after Shiny was taken away, I busted up someone's home, me and some other kids. We poured milk on the walls. It was so old, it stuck. There were fifty of us there in an afternoon. Most of us wore black clothes, hot in the summertime. I saw my face in a mirror. We smoked cigarettes all day long. There was a baby in the bedroom. Someone said that a girl had sucked on the baby to stop him crying. I remembered, when we left, we all walked out and across the street in a group, black and white, our smoke pushed by the wind. Our arms all moved in a certain, tender unison, relaxed, and defiant. It lasted for one, protected moment.

And now in a small brick building, in a very small town, sitting there, and at night mainly, becoming so bright, it was the small, the tiny things that meant most, smaller and smaller, till it was just the space that became most real, the space that was everything. It was always the same. I knew, that from its point of view, nothing could matter.

CHAPTER 10

"Hey!" I heard.

"Hey, Mister," said behind me, like it came to me along a slack rope. It was like crepe paper. It lit an old, familiar spot, making it, and all things dreamlike. I'd been busy thinking about drinking. It had taken the place of everything: my parents, my lovers, the daylight, childhood sight and sound: my life, Joey-taken by it, us broken, and Cokie. Drinking, and the night I was bitten, came to me:

I dreamt a dream of cats all along my left side, biting me with their sharp teeth, hurting me. I woke myself up. There was still the pain. There was one cat left. He was clinging to me with his claws. He was evil. He was about to sink his skinny, bright teeth into the small of my hand. I reached down to him. I eased him back, pulling him by his neck, slowly back. His little yellow eyes let me, watching, and judging. He let go, but the pain stayed on. They weren't cats, and it wasn't a dream.

"Hey, you!" Something was poking me. I was outside in the cage, in a sunny spot. A stick poked me in my back.

In a little opening of the jail fence, a little boy was poking me. I was sitting on the concrete floor, with my knees drawn up. My back was against the fence. I remembered Shiny's laugh as the boy stuck me in the back. She had a short laugh. Like a bright blue, or red baseball cap on a small head. The jab had the feel of a gun barrel, as well.

I turned around. There was a little boy. He had a too-large cowboy hat on; his ears kept it just above his eyes. He saw out at me. He had on a cowboy suit. It was an outfit. His small hands held a little toy rifle.

"Hi," he said. "Are you a jailbird?"

"Well," I said. "I guess I am. Where'd you hear that word?"

"I hear it all the time. I just live over there." He nodded to back behind him, with his head, keeping the eyes and the gun aimed at me. "We can see you from our house, where we live..."

"How old are you?"

"I'm six," he said.

"Who says it all the time?"

"My Mom, and Dad."

"Do they say what a jailbird is?"

"No. They just say it when they eat and when they pull back the curtains to see. It's people in jail, I know."

"Did they send you down here to shoot me?"

"No. I came down to see you."

"What are you gonna do now?" I asked him.

I put my fingers up to look through, to make him look even smaller. He shrugged his shoulders. They were little.

I asked him his name. "Andy," he said.

I told him, "Andy. Look, hold up your hand – like this – put the rifle down – I ain't going nowhere – and look through your two fingers like this – see how I look real little now?"

"Yeah."

"You can do that to anybody you want to, to make them get small – smaller than you. My sister taught me that."

"What else?"

"Well, you know when the moon looks real big and really near the horizon – near the edge of the world – up near the housetops?"

He just watched me. I was pouring it at him, through the holes in my fence.

"You can look at it through your hand curled up – like this – like it's a little peep-hole, a little telescope – and it will make the moon get little. You can make the world get so small whenever you need to.

"It's all I know. Shiny showed it to me."

"Who's Shiny?"

"My sister."

"I got a sister, too. But she's nuts."

"Oh. One more thing I know – Do you have a mother at home?"

"Yes."

"Well," I started to say, "–well, nothing."

"Ok," he said.

I was facing him, sitting cross-legged. I had put my hands up for him. When I saw my palms, I felt as young as I ever had, as young as a boy.

"You're my prisoner, now. My jailbird. I caught you."

"What'd you catch me doing?" I asked him.

"Lyin'. And stealin'."

"What'd I steal?"

"Money."

"Well, tell me about this money I took - and your sister. Is she really nuts? Huh?"

"Yeah. She makes faces all the time – funny ones. Even when she's sleepin'. I've seen her. Somebody took my mom's money, from her purse."

I asked him, "Do you know a girl named Cokie?"

He squinted his eyes for too long. He forgot about language.

"No," he said.

"Well, I don't know, Andy. I'm pretty tired." His little body got in my mind; I could feel its smallness. I put my hand through the fence. He touched me on the hand with his fingers. Then he turned and ran, ran away to his house where he could look out and see the jailbird in the cage. He got littler and littler. He turned into one of the houses down the way.

That night, I remembered him. He was like me, how I had been, so little and laid out in a small bed, with a sister nearby.

I saw him the next day running back and forth in the yard. His knees were in the grass. He played alone. He disappeared into the backyard, then out again, bursting out, with his hand slapping his open mouth. I couldn't hear him. I could see him through the fence. I rested my forehead against it, making an **X** there.

A faded, gray car pulled up to the house. I thought, "Dad." A young girl got out of the rider's side. I felt her feet touch down on the green, front yard. Her feet were light. She walked without making an imprint. She wore a dress, all one piece, a dark plaid. There was red in it. Straps came over her shoulders, over a white shirt. Her arms seemed to float up and wave in the air, oddly. She looked down the way, towards where I was. Her hair swung; her head was shaking it.

She watched me. I wore the red suit, against the white concrete. I held my breath. I stood up. I put my hand to my forehead, flat, to see her by better. She stood there and the little boy came up to her and watched me too. She put her fingers up to her eye and looked through them, to make me littler than I already was. She held it that way for a short time, while the street ran between us. My heart pounded, wooden.

We stayed like that, with our hands where they were, and each with one by our sides. I knew who she was, then. The girl from the cafe. I'd brought her here from there with me. I started to wave at her, when the little boy jumped and ran into the side yard. She turned and went into her house. At the door, she turned her head, and looked, before she went inside.

She carried something bright and good inside the pocket of her dress.

I took her to bed with me that night.

I thought of the patch of yellow light, her bedroom window, her face in it watching out to where she and I now were – in a little country jail house, wrapped up in each other. She had her thin arms around me, at my waist. She was kind. Her hands held my sides, warm like two mouths.

She made signs, for words and sounds, from her window down the street, to us in the jail together. I watched from high up. I was in between the two places; there was a night-time triangle. She made signs that deaf people do, exaggerated; sometimes she shook in herself. Her eyes would roll up. She looked at me, up close, small with me, and she watched from her yellow-lit window down the street, with her face held closely to it.

She repeated certain words, over and over again. I could see her mouth, her lips forming words, repeating them to herself. *Hail, Mary, full of Grace...*

I put my hand down into the triangle where her bare legs met together. She held them closed together. They were thin. I saw her knees, down under the weak blanket we had. I held my hand there and warmed her. I saw her stomach. It stayed still, and strong. Her chest; it was delicate, it wasn't full, and her ribs led up, along her sides, to the swell of her breasts. They were small, and could have fit inside my hand hold, or inside my mouth. I kissed her between them, and it was hard there. It was a place where she never shook or came apart at.

The Lord is with thee...

Her neck had a little hollow at her throat. I could almost circle her neck with my hand. At her face was some pale music, and her lips were reddened as if she'd been sucking on cherry candy. They had trembled many times, with little quakes.

"Pale and quaking..." she said. It was so still, and dark in ourselves, in the jail bed. She got up to me as close as she could.

"I live down the street from you," she said. "Touch my face, touch me all over."

Blessed art thou among women…

I got inside of her, deep, and pushed deeper. She shook her body, almost violently. I dug inside her deeper; her head shook wildly. She jerked under me, she tore around. Her hips were narrow, and small to hold. They moved back and forth, then hard, up and down. She looked in my eyes, opened her mouth to say, "Do that –" and I heard her voice, young, old, and lost somewhere.

I lay down along her back, later in the long night we had. I watched her from the side. I saw the bars, and the smoked over thin window. She could see them too.

And blessed is the fruit of thy womb…

When I got outside in the day next, I worried I'd look down and see her house burned down.

* * *

She, the bright, lonely girl, pure in memory and in her vastly lit heart, had said the words by herself, day and nights, sometimes while leaning on her yellowy window sill, watching down the street-way, to a different place not so nicely lit, but sad… more lonely, where he was…*And I felt it come into me, a spirit, the Holy Spirit, Mary…something Good, something alive, wonderful, clean, pure, and faultless: an Innocence.*

* * *

On a night, I heard a tapping sound on the window of my cell. It sounded like a quarter being held by a small hand, between two fingers, tapping to not be too loud. I felt someone out there, kneeling down, two knees in the soft ground – hopefully a girl bent down and tapping to say hello. It happened two nights in a row.

That night she was outside there, she inside with me, listening to herself on both sides of the window. Naked on one side, crouched and listening – she had her ear up – dressed on the other side, on her knees.

I tapped back. It stopped. Then started again. I did it again. We did this for ten minutes, with different gaps of quiet, some so long I thought she'd gone away. I held my breath. I pushed my feelings out through the window to her – to whoever it was – her, hoped for. It was the silence between the taps that was sweetest.

Then I heard a short yell, a squeal. A sharp light flashed through my window, straight in and round. Like Shiny's cry, and mother's bullet, it ran through me. I backed up into the far corner. A few minutes later, the man I knew, who had the glass-cut scar in his palm, walked by my cell door. He looked in. I was sitting in the corner, waiting. I held her gaps of sound, now a long quiet one, tight in my hands.

Each day she got closer. A yard closer. She waved at me. She looked at me, both of us small at our distance. She opened her mouth. I could see her teeth. I saw her face, her head, and her body. She walked slowly. She stared. She let her head jerk back; she tried to hold all that inside her. She yelled once, a bright and colored noise, a tiny girl-yell. She held her hands, behind her, then in front. I took her with me to bed every night — and those hands. My mind was so open:

I put my hand to her face. I traced patterns on it, and around her eyes. I put my fingers inside her wherever I could. I put them in her as deep as I could, then she was lying on her stomach. She wore just her shirt and her socks. Her shoes and pants were over in a pile on my floor, a dark floor, with her soft things laying on it. She turned slowly over; she reached down and held my wrist, keeping me inside her. She laid on her back with my hand like a cup, one finger in deep, warm, hidden, making her look at me with half-closed eyes.

She pushed herself harder down on my hand. She brought her legs up, bent at her knees, slightly. She had her head pushing backwards, then her mouth gripped shut, her teeth shut tight. Her eyes went up. She pushed down on me, forcing herself on me harder. I felt the quake down deep inside her, where it was near its source. She wanted me to feel her in there when the seizure began. During it, she went wild, pushing, pumping, crying out, her hands over her mouth, pressing her lips flat, white. Then I lay down on top of her. I covered her until she stopped, and then to rest with her until morning. She was an auburn haired, Catholic, Irish-descent girl, a Saint, who sang tears on her way to Christ, and she had that wild, flown-apart appearance.

When I saw her out in her yard, she walked along the curb top, one foot in front of the other.

* * *

The first day she touched me, I was the only prisoner in jail. She reached in and touched me on the shoulder while I sat in the sun. No one was allowed to communicate with the prisoners that way, out in the cage area. People drove by and yelled. Someone threw a beer bottle at me once. It hit the fence. Now, she was here.

She came up quietly. I heard her shoes; my back was to her. I was afraid for her to see my face up close. I thought I'd made all of it up, and I knew how I looked.

She crouched down to get even with me where I sat. I heard it. I felt her push her skirt down in front, between her knees, down in between.

She had her knees out at me, resting on her feet. Her fingers came through the fence.

"Was that you?" I asked her.

"When?" is the first word I heard from her real-mouth.

"Tapping a quarter at my window?"

"It was a silver dollar I had," she said. Because my back was to her, she talked differently. Her words touched the back of my head. There was another little wind out there. Hers was a young voice, shaped, sounding deeper, and older. It came from somewhere I couldn't tell, inside her. From her throat, darkish, smooth, and rough, too.

And when she spoke I thought maybe I heard a very soft echo of it, just falling in after her words.

"It sounded lighter than a silver dollar," I told her. "And, nice. I liked it a lot."

"Me, too," she said. "I knew you were behind that one. I tapped at the other one, next to yours, but no one answered." I didn't tell her she was with me that night, naked in a gray, jail room, also listening to herself out there in her knelt in dark.

"Did they get you? Did they see you?"

"Yeah. He came up behind me like this," and I felt her gesture at me. "He scared me. But he didn't say anything, just watched me run home." She leaned in closer to me. "I ran, but not to my house – I didn't want him to know. I ran down the alley.

"Turn this way," she said.

"Maybe you shouldn't see me, up close," I said.

"I've seen you already," she said. "Come on."

"Why – why all this?" I asked.

"Because. Just because I want to– don't you? Cause of that night. Because — you were staring at me."

I turned to face her.

She and I saw each other up close. So close. I saw her mouth. I looked there, and I felt her small breathing. I saw her eyes, dark eyes, set in, looking out, boldly, and the harder part under them, brightened.

"I wanted to come down here. It felt like maybe we were already... friends, a little. I don't meet many new people... I guess I'm kind of nervous."

She started to smile.

Then – the fence got hot! Something: electric, I thought, turned on by the cops. Everything went red. She threw her head backwards, and started to yell up at the sky. She clamped her mouth closed hard. She gripped the fence, her fingers turning white, then also red. She strained at it, pulling hard on it. The fence stretched out with her. Then she did scream. I touched her hands at the fence.

"Hey!" I said. "Stop — Hey! What do I do?"

She shook her head from side to side hard and fast. I could hear the twisting sound of her neck, and the shagging sound of her hair. It flew across her face and her open mouth.

"Hey! Hey!" I didn't know what to do, trapped in a cage. I caught her eyes for brief moments. It looked like she was saying *No.* Then she seemed okay.

Two cops came. They grabbed her from behind.

"Help her," I yelled. They pulled her away from me. They sat her down on the cement, away from the wire of the cage – with nothing to hold on to. She still shook her head, like that, slower now, back and forth. Her straight dark hair flowed with it, graceful. They watched her. I saw her dress, her legs, her clothes, each part of her in pieces.

One of them said, "Put something between her teeth."

She yelled at them, "No!" She was settling down. She pulled up her knees against her chest and buried her face in them, coming to a stop.

She slowly dragged her face across her knees, like she was caressing it. Her dark hair stayed fallen in her white face. For a moment we all sat there, quiet out in the sun-lit cement lot. It was white under us as it held her.

She got up and ran as fast as she could, away, away towards

her house, cutting down the alley before reaching it. And she was gone. We watched her. Her arms were held in front of her against herself. When she ran her clothes moved loose around her. I watched her back. I wanted to touch her there. She was running away with the girl who had sat down out there like that. I wanted to carry her.

"What in the hell —?

"Who is that girl?" they asked.

"I don't know," I said. "Really, I don't know. I don't know her."

They watched where she went.

"Inside, Carl. That's enough for today. We'll just let it rain outside for a few days, I think. You can stay inside. That girl could be prosecuted for coming over here, for talking to you, you know - she can read the sign. All right, Carl? You tell her next time."

"Next time," I said. "Next time."

"What was she, anyway, an epileptic or something?"

"I don't know," I said. I waited for him to go away. He waited, too. "She's just a girl that showed up here out of nowhere," I said. "I think she was just upset is all. She's just upset about something," I told him.

CHAPTER 11

I thought about how I'd talked to that girl, felt her words on my neck, and heard her rustling, and putting her hands to the fence. I thought about her dress she had on. How she had pushed it down between her legs so she could crouch down out there behind me. I thought of her mouth, when she talked, and when she must pray, about what had happened to her. I knew she was thinking about me, at her house. I knew she was alone with herself. I knew the horse story from my childhood, of grandfather's, could not be true.

I remembered what it felt like, to be alone most of the time, slanted times usually, and little things, like water dripping on the window sill at my house, and Shiny's twelfth birthday party:

I had to go get her at a movie theater. I went to them all in town - there were only three – to find her. I saw her bike out front, leaned against the wall. Her bike was thick-wheeled, with thick handlebars, more like a boys'. She had ribbons hanging from the hand grips. *shiny* was scratched in the back, rounded fender.

She was sitting by herself next to a wall in the darkest seat she could find, away from the little wall lights. They were shielded and threw the light upwards in triangles. I knew about her, that she would sit there. She sat small in the seat. She had popcorn and a Coke.

I sat behind her for a little while. When I did, she turned part way; her hair moved, even though it was pretty short. She rubbed the back of her neck while I sat there. She sat the Coke down on the arm rest away from her. I watched her hand as she held it there, tested it, and let it stay. I looked at her shoulders, and was aware of her face.

I leaned up and put my face against her neck, resting on her shoulder. I put my hands on the top edge of her seat.

"You're wearing your dress, but you ain't at your party, Shine. How come?"

"I'm wearing a dress, and I ain't at no party — ? You ain't wearing no dress and you ain't at no party – either !"

"Sssh," I said. "Don't you want to go? Mom's sad about it. She got a cake and stuff. There'll be people there."

"Daddy won't be," she said.

"I know – I know," I told her.

"He'll never be again, will he?"

"I guess not."

"And that man called, that man that was crazy last summer, that followed us. Dad gave him our number and invited him to my birthday party – over a year ago. And he called!"

"Ssssh! I know. Mom told me. Let's go. I can't stay long – I didn't pay. I told them I was looking for you. Someone might steal your bike."

"No one would –"

I held her shoulders. I squeezed them, then sat back for awhile. Then we left.

"I'll help you, at the party," I told her.

I didn't help very much. She kept her hand up to her face most of the day. She covered her mouth when she laughed or smiled. I pulled it away. Shiny covered her face. She got red.

I tied a string to her wrist attached to mine. It was about six feet long. We kept it on all day, all night, and until she had to go to a different classroom at school on Monday. We walked to school together that way.

When she took a bath, I sat on the edge of the tub and talked to her.

I said her, "Happy Birthday to you," in the bathroom, way after the party.

"Is the door locked?" She asked.

"Yeah," I said.

"Good. That man – he was so strange. He was so sad. Did you talk to him – about Dad, or anything?"

"A little," I said. I could see her chest, different than it had been, only a few months before; and from mine. She didn't mind. It was wet. She was Shiny, in the bathtub on her birthday.

The man acted like a deaf man. He could speak, but he used his hands most of the time. He could make a world with them.

"Remember how weird it was when he followed us that time?"

I said, "Yeah, it was."

"He told me his whole life story, before he waved Dad off the road. You were asleep."

"Yeah," I said. The man sat at the children's table at Shiny's party. Mom was the only other adult, and then her friend, Libba came. She's the one who found the three of us, later, when she saw Mom dead on the floor.

That string, I remembered. I looked at my wrist, my left wrist. I let Shiny have the right one. She liked that we did that, so much.

The man sat and bit the inside of his mouth all afternoon. He got cake and ice cream, but only ate a little bit of it, one bite. A couple of times he started in his chair whenever anyone said anything to him. He seemed to hold back tears, and wore a sad look all day long. He gave Shiny a present. It was a silver necklace with a medallion on it, with a dog's head on it.

"This is really nice," Shiny said to him. He made a face. "Really," she said. "I like this very much." And she did. She wore it, and it would be somewhere near her now.

"I wish you a very happy birthday, Elizabeth," he said. Everybody looked at him. I touched Shiny on her hand, before it could go up to her mouth.

"Thank you," she said, "and for coming."

We had to sleep in the same bed because of the string. She felt hot and damp under her pajamas. In her sleep, she was worried.

I remembered her, that last birthday of hers we had together. I pressed my gums in bed while she slept, nervous, and up much of the night. I used to press them until they bled. I watched her sleep. She got a guitar that day from our mother. She never played it but once. She strummed it and jerked back her hand and made a face.

Shiny's face. I mopped now and thought of her, and of the new girl I knew, a funny, sad, new person: her standing, making me look even more tiny all the way from her front yard.

I got Shiny a pocket watch for her twelfth birthday, with a chain on it to hook to her belt loop. It was engraved. It was a pretty good one. It just said, "Shiny – love, Carl". I wish I'd said more on it, now, like: "I'll stay young with you."

CHAPTER 12

The one cop, he was my friend.

"Six months, that's not too bad, Carl. You'll be out of here, not too long -"

"It's okay," I said. "I'm safe in here."

"Safe? From what?"

"Just safe."

"Well – I saw your girlfriend today, out in the lot. She was walking by. She was looking for you."

Girlfriend? I thought. I didn't know who that would be.

"Oh –" I said. "Her. She okay?"

"Yeah. I talked to her."

"Really?"

"Yeah. She walked by and she tried to look for you without being seen. But I saw her. So, I called out to her. She stopped and looked at me. She's a funny girl, Carl. I crossed over to her side of the street. She's a pretty girl, though, I got to say. She's epileptic. She told me."

I nodded my head. I held onto the mop handle.

"Says it's not too bad. She has what she called 'mild seizures.' I think she had one while we talked – a real mild one. Just made her look intense, you know, sort of crazy. At first I thought she was playing with me, the face she made. I thought she was making me a fool – but then I looked deeper in her eyes. It was real. It was real, alright. She's got it. She's a sweet kid."

I closed my eyes.

"She said she hoped – no – she 'wished you well,' and hoped you were doing okay. I told her not to worry."

"Hmmm," I made a noise. "Yeah, well..." I didn't remember if she knew my name.

"Carl. I told her she could come inside and visit you. On Thursdays. Come in like regular visitors do. I invited her for you."

"What'd she say?"

"She said, maybe. Maybe she would. She will. I told her to look out for that fence stuff in the future –"

"Thanks, Bob," I said. "I appreciate it."

On Thursday, she was there.

We met our visitors right out in the entrance area of the Police station. There was a new guy, and his family was there. They all seemed to have on stretch pants, pink and green colors, with knap on them. They all had a lot of teeth. His grand-mother was there; she was straining to hear, to try and understand.

And Rachel; she sat with her legs tight together at her knees, with shorts on. They were yellow. She held her hands together in her lap. Her head was down. She was looking at her hands, without knowing it. Her lips were tightened, into her mouth. She sat like a little girl in a boat, in a row boat on one of the wooden cross seats, alone in a big sea.

I sat down beside her. We didn't look at each other, but we knew. When she came in, I wondered if she asked for me. She must've, in some way. My friend, he might've seen her there, asked her to sit and wait. He didn't talk to me much, but looked. He was a quiet man with the pain on his face like a rough complexion.

"Hi," I said. My leg was just up against hers. We sat next to each other on the bench. We leaned back against a green-painted wall. It was too late for us to not be there, or anywhere, together.

"Hi," she said back. She coughed a little. We were so quiet. She still looked down. I looked where she looked.

"You okay?" I asked her. I remembered how she'd looked, that day.

"I'm fine." She clenched her face slightly. She swallowed. She faced me. She didn't outright, but she had on a slight smile. "You okay?" she asked.

"Yeah," I said. "Thanks."

"So where were we?" she said. "When I so rudely – interrupted us," and she laughed, small.

"You know, my brother told me about you," she said. "I didn't know – I mean, I just thought, and then I saw you down here, from my house, and it just seemed like —"

"I know," I said.

"I remembered," she started, "I remembered you, how you looked at me that night at Torino's. How you were... How you just sat there and stared at me. Something – about you - and something, about me."

"I remember," I said. I looked at her shorts where her legs came out. "I thought about you, just the stuff I knew. There's not that much I know, so I had to make some up. I had to imagine you," I said. My hands in my lap looked completely inseparable.

"That's nice," she said. "I was drawn to come down here, to see you," she said. "I just wanted to. I liked it that night, when you watched me. I– I'm sorry – How long do you have to be in here?" she asked.

"About five more months, I think. Don't be sorry."

"Oh, I don't mean I'm sorry, I just wanted to come down –"

she said. "Five months isn't too bad...."

"I guess it's not. I almost like it," I told her. I wasn't sure what to do much anymore, out there." She was like a young mother, a small one.

"Sometimes it is pretty hard, to know," she said. "I keep waiting to know what I'm doing here – but I think maybe I'll survive. You, too."

"Yeah, well, you mainly –"

"Everybody," she said. She looked over at the grandmother. She was looking around. "It's whatever you have to do, can be so hard," she said. "I don't always know why, or understand my purpose," and after a moment or so, she twitched along the side of her face.

"I think about you," I said. "I can't stop. I don't stop. When you're at home, in bed, asleep."

"I'm never really very asleep," she said.

"Well then, late at night, and other times."

"That's nice." She wrung her hands together. It made red creases a little. Then we looked at each other. I thought of the blacked out pieces in my head, with only a few, early, clear pictures to draw from.

Her eyes, then, were like my own, how I'd seen them in my mirror when I was most lost, without Shiny, a long time back, and living in homes I hated, without Joey yet, or even little Cokie, or myself.

"I'm older than I look," she said.

She shivered; she eased her head back. She took a deep breath through her mouth. She held herself with her arms. She wore a small, yellow picture of someone on her shirt.

"Who's that, on your shirt?" I asked her.

She said something, "It's a pin, of St. Jude," and just then I remembered all the years gone by so fast, since Shiny. It was the face of someone, on her shirt that did it, the remembering that time when the gesturing man sat at Shiny's party table. It came to me now, like a piece in an old dream. He gave her that picture of a dog's head on a chain to wear.

Was it buried with her now deep inside the holy ground of her?

"I like it," I said.

"Thank you," she said. Her eyes grew bigger, and she had waves, at times a whole wild lake in her. I put my hand against her leg, just above her knee. She was shaky, and trembled a little. She held her feet on tip toes.

"I missed you," I told her, "those days I was inside."

She looked sad, more tired and a little blushed.

"What's it like, for you," I asked her.

"I can't tell you now," she said. "Sometime, okay?"

"What's your name?" I said.

"Yours first."

"Carl," I told her. "A stupid name. It's a fat man's name."

"No, it's not. It's like a grape drink, out of a glass bottle, a Nehi drink. From Ollhoff's. That first taste is the dirt on the lip," she said.

"Carl what?"

"Apalaris."

"I'm Rachel Coyne," she said. "Do you want to come over?" We laughed, on the bench. There was the echo again when she laughed. I looked at it.

"Maybe," I said. "Probably."

She put her smaller hand, held in a half-closed way, in between our legs, too, barely touching.

"So, what'd you do to have to get put in here - Carl?"

"Not too much. I broke a big window, and, before, something at someone's house – no big stuff. I'm not a big criminal.

"*Rachel's* nice," I said. I thought of a garden, somewhere. "It's a red name." I told her. "I like colors, and yours is definitely red, I think. Maybe cause of the 'R.' What's your middle name – got one?"

"Kim. No one has ever called me that, though."

"You like it?"

"It's okay. I keep it to myself usually."

"I could call you Kim, too, sometimes. Okay?"

"Okay."

Before she left, she struggled. She was like bones, held inside, all separate in her. She struggled with her hands.

She sort of held them up and a little over at me. She opened them halfway. She held them at heart level. They might have shaken some. They wanted to hold something.

"I want to know you," I said.

"Yeah, I want to know you, too," she said. "I have so much to tell you, that I want to tell you, if I can."

"Me, too," I said. "Me, too."

CHAPTER 13

Once, only once, Shiny and I went to the Drive-In. Mom had a date, so we had to go out. The Drive-In was only a few blocks away. It was next to a cornfield and a swimming hole. There were always a lot of people there, yelling and playing games, never just being there.

You had to walk a long way in the corn furrows to get to it, too. It was hot and dirty and sticky, and stupid. Shiny went; she didn't mind. Her hair used to stick out. I remembered seeing it from behind her, walking in the dirt, in the summer. Those kinds of pictures in my mind – they were different than the way it really was, it being only a memory.

We sat at nights with other people we never talked to, out there in the cornfield's edge, and would watch movies at the distance. We could see the whole Drive-In from where we were, and the screen shining out to us. Sometimes Shiny'd talk to other people, but I didn't want to. One time she cried at what she saw on the screen, at a distance, without any sound hardly getting to us. She sat on the ground without her shoes on, and cried into her hands at what the actors did. It was what they did to some animals. That ground, it's still out there that held her small weight like it was nothing. All the people having walked out there now that are gone.

She always said how the animals weren't acting. "I know they kill them, just for a movie," she said. "They don't care. And when those horses fall down like that – they break their legs all the time – I know they do."

One time Sammy Davis Jr. was in a show and someone shot his cow, or a bull, in a dusty cowboy street, and Shiny cried, and tore her shirt over it. She cried harder at that than I'd ever seen her.

* * *

I held Rachel-Kim to go to sleep at night, and she went to sleep too. I held on, and tried not to remember how big everything was, and how far away someone could get from you, if you let go. I opened her shirt to get to her chest. She would say, "Carl," or, once, "Carl, I feel one, coming."

"What?"

"You know."

Then she'd have a seizure, or an orgasm. I put my mouth against her; it could slide, or move on her. I pressed her flat against her chest with my hand, till the quake went away. Maybe her seizures were like orgasms running through her body like waves running through, coming like a timed rhythm, building until they took over. And in that being taken over, she got to let go, let herself be flung out and away from what was usually held in tight. She was lucky. An eruption, and a peace, then going black into a closed up closet inside, with a beat and some lightning flashes, too.

She said, "It's not regular epilepsy, it's just some fits I have."

Sometimes I put my mouth down between her legs, open, and pressed on, and held while she went into it. That way, I could be with her. She bucked, it got hotter, and she tasted different then, acidy, and sugary. Then, when she stopped, I tasted everything she had out of her, almost till blood came. I held her and held her, everyway I could think of: hands pushed under her arms, under the small of her back, under and around her neck, and her head – and how it was small in my hands. I pet her. I held her face, I held around her waist, under her hips, between her legs, and at her chest, and her stomach.

My mouth found its way to wherever she was. I put it on her for long times, and pushing in and out, licking and kissing and being there so dear and it being bright too, and she would heat up, and get wild, and shine like tinfoil, and twist herself. She laughed, and shot everywhere happiness, and hot tin girl…

…and Hail, Mary, full of Grace, the Lord is with her… nightly in her peace while I roamed her spirit and body and heart, from such a Holy distance, together, mind, body, soul, me, Shiny and now, Rachel Coyne…

* * *

That one time we went in and paid, at the Drive-In, Mom gave us the money to. We had to walk, and get in the line with the cars, moving slow, holding hands against them, and the faces and horns. We went in, me and Shiny, and sat on the bench they had, and watched, and ate, and had Cokes. That night I was thirteen. I felt how Shiny, on the bench with me, was thinned out inside herself, and how she drew odd people around her, and how she herself was alone down inside her. I got scared for her, for what was coming from her future, like stones, and like she might be crushed, and disappear under it. I put my arm around her. She was my sister. She had the same-blood running, going through her, under our skin. Hers had different messages than mine, but almost the same, and I loved her so.

I hugged her, and she let me. She said, "yeahhh," real slow through her lips, when she felt relaxed. She leaned against me, until it got cold out. The movie was lost to us anyway. We got up and walked back home.

* * *

One time I saw Shiny dancing in her room. She saw me, too. I came in as she danced; she shook her whole body all at once, holding her face a certain way to do it, then stopping. She smiled at me, and then jumped; she jumped all over her room. She jumped at the walls. She made me laugh.

Shiny: she was Carl's sister – she made me laugh that day cause she danced in her room for me like an epileptic girl gone wild. She said she wanted three colored stripes on her face, below her eye running along her upper cheekbone, disappearing into her hair where a sideburn would've been. They would have to run across her temple.

"Three different colors, red, blue, and maybe bright yellow, or some mix of other colors," she said. "I feel like they belong there. They are there but you can't see them. You can feel them, though." And she told me to touch there on her face, to feel them.

"When I get older," she said, "I'm gonna get them painted on, or tattooed, or whatever it takes to make them stay. I could cover them with make-up later, if I ever wanted to, but every morning I got up, they'd be there to see in the mirror."

I could've run ads in papers around the country looking for a girl with three stripes on her face, but I never did, yet. She had a certain smell on her, too. Her voice always surprised me. Almost every time she spoke it gave me a little shock at how familiar it was, how it had a little hit in it, a push, a spark. She spoke to me a thousand times.

I thought of those times, sitting in the shadows of jail. I wanted to get a knife and cut out the last twenty-five years of my memory. I could give the knife to Rachel to use, or to

Shiny: girls with knives.

"I don't like what I did, what I am," I said to Rachel, in our made up night time together. Maybe I can pretend, I thought, to have had a real life. Maybe I only went to a couple of schools, and like a regular boy, to the dances, and was at the group events; I had friends, and a place to live in I liked a lot. I see myself there: I'm laughing, look Rachel, laughing: I'm touching someone. I'm sleeping through an entire night. I'm young, and I'm good, I'm not afraid, I'm not alone. I'm thinking about bright things and funny - me, I'm here, and there's no girl here when I'm a man, with a shape on her back, a young girl with a Coke bottle in her name.

* * *

There'd been a few times, nice ones, Friday nights some-times when the phone would ring, and the house was lit up warm and yellow. I had a friend or two. I watched Shiny's face while she watched me talk. When I listened, I looked to her, and asked her with my face, what she wanted. She wanted to be in whatever there was around. Sometimes I heard her whistling at things, things outside her window, even things she had hung up on her wall, she'd whistle at. She danced to her own whis-tling, slow, and with her eyes closed.

I stood in line with Shiny. I held her at her waist, above her narrow hips, and she swayed some, foot to foot, while we waited. She held onto my belt-loop, with her finger, whenever she was behind me.

CHAPTER 14

My house, alone, was like a man with his eyes closed, its heart was broke. It sat with its wounds and with its holes. It held a few precious things, mainly pretense. There was a picture of Jesus, with light on his face. His chest was soft white. A small picture, in a frame, and in a fire, set by me, I'd grab it.

Cokie asked me, "Who's that guy?"

"Guy?" I said. "That's God –"

"God? How's that?"

"What? You've heard of Jesus –?"

And she said "No."

"Well, as unbelievable as that is, this is like a picture of a young God, a teenaged God."

She laughed; she didn't have one line on her face, except when she laughed or cried. Sometimes she cried in my house, just sat and cried, with her face wide open to me. "I've heard of Jesus." she said.

"Well, you know, I like Him. He loved everybody. He couldn't help it, even the people who nailed Him to a cross. Most people don't care, don't ever even think about it, like it doesn't matter anymore. But it does."

"Men did that," she said.

"Yeah. He loved them, and He forgave them even right then when they were doing it."

"Do you love me?" she asked.

"I do love you. I love you, like I do, as you are. You're a young girl, a friend of mine now. I hope He forgives me," I said.

"For what?" she said. She stuck out at me, sitting there.

"You," I said. "For you. Shoot, I wish — well, for you. For spoiling you..."

"You never spoiled me. What'd you mean – spoiled?"

"Spoiled – I mean – that maybe we did things together, before you, or me, should have. See?"

"What? What things?"

"Like, I drank your body like a river. I touched you. Let's be honest – dear – listen, you're so sweet – that I was close to you – that... you're so nice..." and so I couldn't, I couldn't let her know.

"Yeah? What - what'd you do, that you need God - the teenaged God, to forgive you? What'd you do to me that was ever wrong?" She turned up her face to me.

Then, she was a woman. "Nothing," I said. "Never mind it."

Sometimes other people came over, and then they never came back, and years now passed. My sister was my only love. I had some of her old stuff in a drawer of mine. There was a black and white picture of me and Shiny and my mom and dad by an old Christmas tree, back in the 1950's.

* * *

Where I had put my fingers; what they had touched. With them, and with colors I was given, I drew some pictures of people on some paper, in jail.

I drew them according to what I liked about them. I showed Shiny with big eyes, a small mouth, and a little waist. I imagined her with her hands covering her ears, but I didn't want to draw that at all. Her chest was a place to write something. I wrote *mercy*. I'd read that if God ever punished people, or even the devil, there was always a time lag involved to it, so that people maybe had time to repair or be sorry for what they'd done, and to be forgiven. I figured it would be better to kill someone rather than yourself, cause then during that merciful time you could make up for it, maybe by helping other people. The dead person would be okay, because they'd be okay somewhere, like heaven, or nowhere, depending on whether there was a God and all that anyway. So, I drew it on the place where Shiny's heart would be.

When it rained, I drew the faces. And at night, I did it, by a single light bulb. It was quiet and when I lay down, turning from my back to my side, I wasn't as alone in there. Shiny, and Cokie, not Joey, and Rachel were on the paper – it wasn't newspaper – and some others, and I knew Rachel was sleeping with me, too, down at her house down the street.

In the night, the pictures were still there as much, but in the dark they just couldn't be seen. I slept in the night with my watch on. I heard Shiny sing in the picture of her I painted in gaudy blues and yellows.

And: In the night, I woke up, I gagged, choking on vomit in my throat. I sat up. There were tears in my eyes. I looked around. 'Where am I?' I thought. 'Oh, God! Where am I?'

CHAPTER 15

In the morning, it felt like it had snowed outside. The light was muted. The sounds were faded, even the footsteps in the jailer's room, and the radio voices. It was cold. I laid there. I knew,

"She might wander over to me. She might be wearing a dress for me, again, yellow, or red with yellow, her hands stuck out below the cuffs."

I ate breakfast, and drank the black coffee. I let some syrup drip down into it, to sweeten it. It was warm in my mouth. I watched my hand hold onto the coffee cup. I liked my hands. I marveled at them, that they existed. They looked so odd. I held them at my mouth and tasted what I called Rachel on them.

* * *

There was a chapel over at the college I'd walked to at night. Cokie and I walked there in the day. She ran at me when she saw me, by the corner grocery. She jumped up on me, wrapping her legs around me. She pushed her smaller face against the side of mine, hard boned and warmed. Her hands grabbed behind my neck.

"Carl!" she'd say. "God," she said, so dear, and guts. "Oh, Gaahd – Carl..."

She squeezed her eyes shut hard. I pretended to others,

inside me, that she was my daughter being raised by another man and my ex- wife. And him being a strict, dark man, bigger, stronger than me, keeping me from her, and that's why I could look and be happy, and sad, to see her, and hold her hand to walk down to the campus and the chapel there.

It had an outside hallway with cut out windows, cut into thick stone walls. We sat on the ledges together and watched the students go by. We draped our legs over. Hers were shorter, and she wore blue pants. With some buttons.

"Think anybody knows what we've done, Carl? Huh? Think any of these people can see it in us – in how we're sitting, or on our faces? Huh?"

"No," I told her, "no one. No one knows. I don't even know, really. Do you?" I didn't let her answer.

"I mean, it always happens, so weird, and like it's not going to, and you – you act like – and then something sort of happens, and then it stops, it doesn't happen, and then next thing you know, it does, and it just does – and then it's over and we're talking, or sitting there, or here, and it seems so distant and like never. You know?"

"Wow –" she said. "I think about it, at home, in bed at night by myself."

"You do? Is it good, or bad?" I asked her. When I went there, later, to that ledge place, by myself, I sat where Cokie'd sat.

"Okay," she said. "It's just kissing, anyway. Like kissing. When I'm alone, and when it's just getting dark – I almost scream. I hate that time. I'm used to it, but when it gets dark out, I get loose inside, and in pieces, and kind of scared. Then I like to be in a room with no windows. You come into my mind then. My mom has a little sewing room like that. That's where I go."

I walked all over that campus. It's small, for a college. There weren't that many students. They looked funny.

I worked there, in the kitchen, in the dishroom. I quit. I

was there for a few hours, and I shook. I tried, but I was scared of them. It made me sweat, and then I hated them. I slipped and fell in the wet, and I left. I remembered taking off my apron, and walking home. I walked fast, trying not to run. I got near my house, I got alone. Then I felt better. When I got home, I went in and closed the door, and I never came outside again.

When I'd walked around their campus, no one noticed me. But I noticed them. Them, the same ones in the same places and clothes. But none of them ever noticed me, I was sure.

* * *

My father died. He must have, a long time ago. No one ever told me. My cradle must have been like a jail. In it, I waited for Shiny to be born. Dad invited that crazy man to our house, on her twelfth birthday party. But Dad didn't come himself.

The man was the saddest man, sitting at the children's birthday table, always trying, wanting to get her attention. He waved at Shiny while she acted normal, and was talking, or playing, or eating her cake. He waved by the side of his face.

He didn't know about how she was sitting alone in a movie theater earlier, or about how she was to me, how she was my savior. It was the only time he ever came over. We didn't live there anymore, much after that time. He was a man lost in Shiny. He probably missed her even after he was dead somewhere.

Me, too. Then I thought of Teresa in her car, and how soft and full of juice her skin was, her chest she offered me, as a cruel thing. Her red, thick lips. Her mouth. She saw me as a lie, but with warm hands she put me against her heart, a sweet covering for me.

I missed other people, and things, but it didn't matter. No one knew me well enough to know where, or who I was.

* * *

Before I got up, to wait in the mornings, to go out and wait there for Rachel to come by, I thought about blood. There was so much blood, like lakes, so much blood around. I needed to bow down to something, to blood. It had to be precious.

I thought about how red it looked on skin, or spilled out on the grass or on the pavement. I woke up once in a farmer's field – it was so big, it was all I could see, from my laid down ground level, when I turned my head around. I was in a shallow place in the ground, and when the sun woke me up, there was blood frozen on my face in two long lines, out my nose down to my mouth and chin.

I'd hit myself in the face with a thin, cheap bottle out in a farmer's field. It had been so big to wake up in that morning, with blood, and glass.

I wanted to get down on the floor and adore something. No one had touched me, even on my arm, for a long time – but Him, He had, many times, and I had ignored it. He was the best person in the world that ever lived. He had all the peoples' blood that ever lived, on His hands. He touched everywhere with Kindness all at once.

I missed the farmer's dirt-field. I knew that a lot of jailed people got homemade tattoos that spelled 'Jesus.'

* * *

My mother – we came in from school one day; she was stripping two chairs, straight-backed ones. They sat on news-paper. She used lye to strip them.

"Why – what are you doing?" asked Shiny. "Look at your hands, Mom -"

The lye had burned into them. They almost smoked. She had no gloves on. There were lye-burned spots on her black sweater and on her long pants. She was barefoot in the back, pantry area. She sat on her side, on her hip.

"Mom!" Her hands were red, and tender hot.

"Stop doing it!" I told her. "Get up. Wash your hands – look at them!" Then we were all looking at them.

"Your father has left, you know. Did you know that?"

We looked at her. I looked away. "He left awhile ago, Mom. Mom?"

"Well, you should know, kids, you have to know why. Men are run by their desire – do you know that? Surely you do by now. I know you've seen – they're run by their bloody desires - so he's left us. He left you, too, you know. Not just me. It wasn't just me –"

Shiny closed her eyes, still standing there.

"Mom," I said. "Don't. Just stop working on that chair." She held an arm across her chest.

Shiny opened her eyes. "Look at your hands – please!"

"It's nothing, dear. It's not important. I wouldn't have him back on a Christmas tree. I would not."

Her heart, smeared with lye, burned past the surface red layer of it, was cut, down to the bareness of it, with a smoking-pain.

Up in our rooms we talked, quieter than usual.

"She'll be okay. I mean, the lye, it'll be okay," I said.

"I think so, too," she said. We sat together, as it started to get dark out. We didn't hear anything from downstairs. Shiny turned on a lamp she liked. It had a little horse's head on it. She was too big for that, but she liked it anyway.

Then she said, "I wrote a story today, in school. I had to. It was about the wind, if it started blowing hard, and gusty, and paper blowing and people walking bent over at that angle, headed into the wind, and hats blowing off and trees bent and all that kind of thing happening. And it doesn't end. It just keeps blowing about sixty miles per hour – every day and night, week to week, month to month, year to year. Every time you opened the front door, the wind would just about knock you down. It wouldn't be fun to go outside anymore. It wouldn't matter if you were poor or fat or anything. As soon as you went outside it was the same for everybody – and it got worse and worse. I can just see all the people inside, sitting in chairs, waiting for the wind to die down. But it never would. Outside it would be like a dustbowl, just the wind blowing, even trees, and tables and record players and stuff along in it.

"And it would stay that way and people would have to start living different. Eventually the world would be worn down smaller and smaller, into a tiny, little round place. It would only hold a few people, and a couple of houses. Maybe three people in the end. Me and you and somebody else... I'd like to go to a place where that could happen for us, and it'd be okay, and not bad, and do it as long or as short as we like – where we could do anything. In the story I said, 'my brother.' I didn't use your real name or anything."

I listened.

"We talked about Khrushchev today," she said. "He's the Russian president. He's visiting America." In her voice, sitting there now in my mind's eye, she was the best thing in the whole country. "Someone said that if he fell down somewhere here, and broke his arm, that there'd be a nuclear war."

CHAPTER 16

I saw Rachel coming. I stood up. I had five months left to be here. I stood up straight to meet her.

'I know you, I know you, I know you – let me know you.' *maybe I AM you…* I spoke with my lips on the cyclone fence. She came. It could work, I thought. We could run away. I can have her. There's such familiarity…

I used to stay up all night in my house, alone.

I used to ask the Virgin Mary there sometimes. I was a retarded heart. I took refuge in a child's.

But was I really alone, separate from all the rest, out there? Or what it the other way around? Weren't we all the same, inside? Was there only one, appearing as the many, as I often read and wanted, tried to believe. But I felt so alone.

She came closer towards my fence.

"Dear Mary, Mother of God –" I whispered.

"Hi," she said. "You're outside today –"

"Yeah. They let me come out. They said it was raining the last few days."

"It didn't at all."

"I know. But, now, it means they'll let you come see me out here. You never know what they'll do though –"

"Let me ask you something," she said.

"What?"

"I want you to come over to my house for lunch. We could have sandwiches, and chips, and Cokes."

"I don't know," I said. "Maybe. I'll have to ask," I laughed. "I'll ask my Mom."

I thought of my Mother, coughing, and clicking her high heels in the grocery stores; I'd hear her coming. We were lying down and waiting for her in the backseat of the car, me and Shiny. We carried brown grocery bags into the house.

"There's nothing better than a well-made sandwich," Rachel said.

I agreed.

She stuck her fingers in the fence at me. I wanted to put them in my mouth.

"It would be fun," I said. "We could ride around in a car, and I would just look at you – you'd look little, at the wheel, with the huge background going by."

"Do you just think of me, or am I real to you?"

She seemed to repeat the words in her mouth, as an echo. And like click sounds while she waited.

"Both," I said. "A lot in thoughts – pretty clear. All I really know is the expression I read, "I AM I. It seemed to free me some from all the boundaries and fear, but then I'd be right back."

"I see."

It was her tongue, moving around in there.

"I can feel myself at night, when I dream, being pulled out and away – drawn to you. We do things, don't we?"

"Yeah," I told her.

"You can say *I am I*, and I can say *I am I*, and maybe it's the same I?"

"Yes, maybe… I like that notion so much…Rachel."

She came so close I could've touched her two front teeth in her mouth.

"Are those baby teeth in your mouth, the two little ones,

there – next to the front ones-?"

"Yeah," she said. "They are.

"I have new kinds of dreams, lately," she said. Her fingers were against the fence, down now by her thighs. They were pretty, with the thin, connecting finger bones, little warm, hollow rods in her, sweetly pulled through.

I looked over her shoulder. I saw a man in a sweatshirt with the hood up, pulling a girl up from the street into the back of a pick-up truck, over the back door of it. He pulled her by her arms, too hard. The thin heart of her, out there being pulled up into a truck. But I couldn't see her face.

"Look," I nodded.

She looked. "Yeah," she said, "a picture – her being halfway up – look at her hair."

Then she said to me, "I was never a little girl. I was so scared, and so twisted. It was worse back then." She made the same face the other little girl probably made half way into the truck.

Rachel walked over here everyday to be with us, and we said, smiling, *I AM I*, with her breath going in and out of her. It seemed hard for her. In her miles of nerves, and flashing energy, she was made different; there were explosions in her brain. Her young hands held themselves out at me, resting on our fence in between.

I imagined her asleep on a train, her face laid down in her hand.

"You know, we have all the time in the world —" Rachel said. My head felt big then. I thought of a place I used to be with Shiny, in a wooded place.

"I wanted to talk to you that night at Torino's," she said. "But I couldn't. I didn't know how."

"It was the end of something so big for me," I said.

"I was with my Mom, and her sister - my aunt. They're pretty protective of me."

"Do you take medicine?"

"Yeah, sometimes. Keeps me even. I have mild epilepsy – did you know?"

"I guess I did. It seemed like you did. I liked watching you that night. You were great. I thought you were pretending, just playing around with everybody. You were amazing."

"I know. You stared at me. You looked smaller, and darker then. You were a worry over there to me, I think to everyone. I think people worry about you, about everything in their lives when they see you. Do you think that?"

"Yeah, I feel that, sometimes. But I can't really know."

"We're safe to like each other if we want to. Because you're in here, it's easy. And I want to," she said.

I was quiet. "What were you saying about your dreams?"

"Nothing, no big thing," she said. "It's just strange. It's like, in my dreams, me, the main person, has memories in the dream, and I think they're of other dreams I've had. But maybe, they're just other parts of the dream, like a dreamed up memory within my dreamed up dreamer. But they feel so familiar, like - 'yeah, I remember these people, those faces, and places.' Like this one particular house and all of us are inside it, on a loft, up top, and looking out of it from an opened wall. It's real to me now, but it was an old dream, not a real place. Do you have that?"

"Who's 'us'?"

"I don't know who. Just people that are always there... Joseph and Mary."

I knew I wasn't in her dreamed memories within the dreamer that was her. There's where the bright red would be found. She was like young fireworks.

"Rachel," I said. I put my mouth up to the fence. "I want to come for lunch. I don't want to be with just me or here anymore. I want to come outside with you."

I imagined her throwing a rock, on a dirt road, bending over to pick it up first. She'd throw it funny, and smile sideways at me when she gave. 'Just stay like that, just stay that way forever.'

"Do it," she said. "Like the dreams. Kiss my mouth." I kissed her on her mouth through the cyclone fence. I tasted her – it was small, and warm, and sweet. I wanted it sweet, like a cartoon. She had all of her in there. She never shook. I remembered our nights of love-making, and her seizure when I was inside her body. She held her mouth on me, as still as the ground. I hid my whole past and now short-present in her mouth. She swallowed me into her small head.

* * *

There would always be a blind spot. I was in it almost completely. I felt cold on its edges. I remembered hiding in my foster homes whenever other people came over.

"Hey! Apalaris. Where are you - under the bed?"

"Here, I'm here - in the shadows," I said. "Here, in the shadow of a dead horse. The history of the world is in the shadow of a horse."

"What?"

"Nothing."

"Your friend's here. She's outside."

yes, in all her red-splendid beauty and small

"She's pretty young isn't she? To be hanging around out there. I shouldn't let her, but you're not much of a risk, or her either. I don't mind too much. You going out?"

"No," I said. "I can't today." I thought of how she was the day before. It wouldn't be the same.

"She's out there. She's only out there for you." At this he looked back behind him. "She's standing out by the fence... looking at her feet.

"I mentioned her to the other guys. They saw her – that first day. Hard to be mad at a girl like that."

'A girl like that,' I thought. 'A girl like that.' Her breasts, were small, and like a pink inflamed place, like distant-fun, so bright there. Her face shined above them. I looked at her so hard.

"Come on, Carl, you got a visitor!"

"No! I can't. I don't want to. Just bring me a picture of her. Don't ask me anything." I pulled in close to the blind spot. I saw her face waiting. I couldn't go. She might sing, out there.

She could put her hands under her dress, flat against her thighs. Her wrists would hold up the cotton, colored cloth, slightly.

I got down in the shadows of the blind, and kissed her lips.

I have to stop everything, I knew. Everything I was. All my past. Because of this I have to stop everything. Because of her.

I have been mean, and by myself. I want to come out. I have to forgive something.

She must've waited for me, outside, but she knew I wasn't just inside. She could find me somewhere else. She went home and held herself. She laid down, maybe in her dress, with her shoes on, curled up on her bed, deep in a corner too.

Let me sink into your horror, and oh, you be honest, let me into your dear, dark, sweet girl as mother. Oh, please take my hands, extend yourself. Oh, for gratitude: I am here, I am here thinking of you.

* * *

Through the fence, we talked.

"The only issue is death," I told her.

"Or the other way around, maybe," she said. "Remember: I AM I!"

"Yes. The other day, in the shower, I thought, that I'd miss you, this place of you, if I wasn't here, anywhere... It scared me.

She made a face.

"In the end, I know I'll wish I'd done something. Taken

part. Talked - I should have talked. I should've danced."

She laughed at me. "You're so funny." She knew more than me, more than I ever would.

"I'm here," she said.

"Are you?"

"Yes."

"I know you are," I said. "And on a good day."

"Yes," she said.

"Maybe that's enough," I said, "a nice day. That's probably it."

"I hide my face all the time, you can imagine I do."

"God, I get such a rush for you!" I said.

She laughed in her mouth. I could put my hand, part of my hand in there, like a red, wet place. We were on the cement together, sitting.

"We need spoons," I said.

"Kiss me," she said, "kiss it." She licked, quickly, her two front teeth, as if she had lipstick on them, like I'd seen women do when they had it on their white teeth, but she didn't, she just licked. I held my mouth like she did, mouth to mouth, with the cold reminder of wire pressing in.

I thought in that pressing, to push my hands through the fence and touch her, like I thought no one else ever had but me. Or to push the fence out to touch her. Her chest would stick through the gaps in places, smooth, cotton covered. She was a girl pressed some there already anyway, towards me.

She knew what I thought then, and she came up closer, leaned in with the top half of her. She sat up, onto her knees. I was in jail. She straightened her back. I thought: 'horse's hard back – a small horse – my grandfather's horse – what a liar he had to be.'

Her chest, it did press against the fence. I put my palms there. She wore a thin sweater. I felt her just barely. I touched slightly, her brought-forward heat.

CHAPTER 17

Rachel Coyne had an old sheet of paper at home, folded under in a little box, story-like, that she had written:

'I reached up and behind my head with small fingers. I remember how they were small, small enough to put them through the little window of the metal painted and sculptured tin gas station my Daddy brought home to me one night. A Texaco station. I reached up and touched my favorite dress that hung where I knew it did. I fingered it. It was another person, it, she, was a girl like me. She had all the sweetness and good parts I would have had, if I hadn't been me. I loved her. I do. She was also like a guard. She takes care of me in here. She was always, almost always in here. And when I wore her outside, and to school and places – we went out together.

'I had a whole group of people in there. I had red dress – she was haughty-pretty, and sometimes mean-cold. "Don't," it said, "don't always have to cry in here. Stop being like a cry-baby."

'I had old brown; she was oldest. I could bury my face in her and cry all I wanted to. She didn't get to do much anymore. She was like a donkey.

'There were thin-girls, and fat sweater ones, pretty, and not pretty, and messy, and smelly ones, and there were places to sit on that were better than others, in soft piles on the closet floor for me.

'This is where my seat fits,' I thought, I said out loud. It was warm and I thought about my Daddy. He didn't know I was in here. He didn't know she put me in here, whenever I had a bad fit. I wrote *Daddy* on the palm of my hand. I had to keep it, and re-draw it everyday so it would stay there to see.

'Mom never believed me. She thought I was being bad; she'd lock me in there whenever I was through.

"STOP IT!" she screamed at me. "I know you can stop it!" She cried about it too. I liked my dark friends, and waiting.'

* * *

We were outside and no one seemed to care. This was the whole world. From high up above, or from a tree across the street, we must've looked funny with high wire between us.

"This is so nice," she said. "Being here. So real. Sometimes I've prayed to God, about you, and about me. I tell Him that I don't know anything. That I'm nothing. I thank Him for that, the most. I ask Him to help, sometimes, because I feel crazy and sick inside –"

"So am I," I said. "It feels like you said, so real. Not like you're something outside of me, like most stuff is, you know. But so important."

"I don't know, maybe God can come down to us. Maybe He likes us, different than us being always alone."

"Just you — you're like a prayer itself."

"Sometimes, if I do pray, it's not in my regular voice. It starts out as my regular, day-to day voice, but then something happens, it changes. It's an angel's. For real, I think."

"When I see you, and even if I think of you, there becomes like a third presence, so alive. Like watching, but more like just being with me, something. I can feel it. I don't know what it is, but it's good, and right. I'd like to always feel it -"

"I know what you mean. And you... you've been imagining

us. And so God heard -"

"Maybe," I said.

"It's not maybe. I know you're with me then. I can feel it." Rachel closed her hands in fists, gently in front of her.

"I don't get anything that has ever happened. But you seem to – you know so much stuff about God –"

"No, I don't. It's the not-knowing that's so good," she said. "The trusting whatever It is. God is good, God is great, God is everywhere. God is in me... Remember that?"

"No," I said. "But I want to...

"Do you have to be able to imagine things first, before they can happen – at least be able to see yourself in a certain situation before they can happen?"

"I don't know," she said. "Sometimes things happen, good, or horrible, without ever thinking of them before at all. I feel so fragile right now. I'm afraid to move." She held tightly to the fence with her small hands.

"If we had a baby… a baby. That'd be a real third presence," I said, out of nowhere.

"Wow –" she said, quietly. I looked at her hands, where they gripped.

"I don't know anything about it hardly," she said. "I'm a virgin, you know, I guess. So it might be easy - to do it, to make it happen." Rachel smiled.

"To impregnate me –" she said the word like a place to travel. She laughed.

"Some ideas are so wrong, cause they aren't ever going to happen. This probably has already happened and we're going to live it, or we wouldn't be thinking, and talking about it," I told her. "I believe that."

"What will we do?" she asked. She asked me that.

"Well, maybe we'll have the baby." I said, from our nights together, hot as summer, sweat and thick, for it to be made in, *Rachel at home saying Holiness between us when it happened.*

She knew. "It will be everything," she said.

"A baby, God, a baby. Such a thing – a separate thing. It's hard to imagine. I maybe always wanted one, a child, maybe like someone…I once knew. I don't know why I said it. Maybe I want to be good to one, to a child. I like the word."

"It might be a girl, I think. If there ever was one," she said. "You'd love her, love her all the time, a child for you. You would hold her and carry her. You could put her down though, from time to time. Or you and me, we could keep her feet from touching the floor for a long, safe time – so it, she, would know that she's loved. We'd become addicted. We'd ask God to help us."

"Can you see yourself without your disease?" I asked her.

She jerked as that went into her mind. Her eyes grew a little. She was willing to give me everything, I knew, even a baby. I knew that. She pressed against the fence for me.

"No," she said. "No, I'm not ready – and that's hard to say – and also, maybe, yes, just maybe."

"No and yes to everything," I say. "Coffee at a cafe: always in a paper cup. 'Put mine in a dirty glass,'" and Rachel laughed.

"We'll start imagining the child," she said. "A little baby in me. And we'll call it that: The baby. We have nothing to lose, either of us. It could already be there, here," she pointed, "inside me. The moment we made it together…through wanting," she murmured. "So, we hold the thought like a clear thing, like a case for something to grow inside…

"I feel different," she said. "I feel large."

I thought of the two of them, her, and her baby, both facing front, their eyes widened, their mouths, openings to minds.

"I'd have to cut myself, start now, start here, cut myself deep, in order to get that kind of happiness." I said.

"No," said Rachel. "No. Don't talk about cutting. There won't be any cutting on either of us, no, no," and she was going to cry. "No, don't make a mess, please, of you, or me. I don't deserve that."

We blew through an empty fence. We had to think something. We were here, after all. Nowhere but here. We watched it. A baby would be here, too, just to love.

A colored string still attached, from a birthday party. Colored smears were shot all over my memory.

I knew, I saw how, years to come, if they did come, all I'd have maybe left of Rachel would be a photo of her, with some red dye bled onto her face from some red paper I'd carried so long next to it, run some onto her face, near her mouth, and down on her shoulder, and gone, her gone by then. Where would the baby be, and how much if any would I be a part of it, maybe just a shape to live with, maybe while she took a solitary walk, she'd wonder about me. She could grow up and fly if she could just hold the thought long enough, dear enough in her, flight guided by an invisible thing like an idea, or feeling of love, and not the shape of a father long ago lost.

* * *

"Where is your sister?" asked Rachel.

"I don't know. They never told me."

"Who didn't?"

"All the people, the foster people and the cops, the people in charge."

"I thought you told me some place, a town, and a name -"

"No name, no name. There was some place, far away, and I could never get to her. I tried to, and that year – that was a long time ago, that was a rough year for me, some things came out."

She didn't say anything to me. She sat and watched, from on her knees. She tossed her hair, hand-cut, jagged, just below chin length.

"It was a time when I sort of let go, and was taken over by

some stuff from our past -"

"Our?"

"Me and Shiny's. Since then, I've lost track of her."

"Shiny. I like to say her name. Say more – was she really so beautiful, to have that name?"

"When I say, or think her name, it feels good. It's like she's inside me. Yeah, she was that beautiful. It was like she was startling to see, every single time I ever looked at her, I was surprised at the clarity, the brightness of her beauty. She was an angel. It was sort of hard for her to be that bright. To carry it around...

"I used to hear Shiny singing outside, from my bedroom window. I used to go to her room, I liked it better there, cause her things were in there, and her hands had touched everything. I looked out her window to see the top of her head. She looked up at me, and stopped singing."

Now I could hear it again. A song inside a girl, lost, and a secret, and talked about to a girl she would never know.

"Well, why do you say, 'was?'"

CHAPTER 18

In the nights were thunderstorms in my cell. It was blue water, with colored fish in it. I saw Rachel, out in the pen, all the time. I saw me in her special light, now. There was also a mother thing on her, a mantle. Jesus' young face is what got me through all those years that were blackened.

The shape was Him. Inside us.

"Mother of Christ," I said. "All women are that, aren't they. What else can they be?"

"A little mother," Rachel said. "I'd like to be that, and to remain good to the baby."

"And how is she today?" I asked her.

"The mother or the baby? Well, she, or he, is okay. I'm fine, too. She's so fine. So safe. She's deep in here," and she held her hands there and her eyes looked down just to that part of herself.

"Our babies – are angels inside us. All I had to do was nothing."

I cleaned all the building that morning. Sometimes I watched TV. I was still alone, mostly. Sometimes there were short timers in for awhile. Out town was small; we all knew each other, even if we didn't. On the TV all the people looked alike.

Rachel's little brother, Andy, came over again. He had a loose tooth. He showed me how it was almost hanging.

He smiled around his loose tooth.

He pushed at it with his tongue, then hard from behind it. It came out. It was little. "Is it bleeding?" he asked.

I looked at it, and it was. "Let me get you something," I said. "Stay here."

I went into my cell and got him a tin cup of water. He drank it down and rinsed with it. I poured it down to him through the cyclone fence. He liked doing it that way.

"I have my yellow cap on," he said. His other teeth clicked on the rim of the tin. I could smell how tin made the water taste, and with the little blood in it, too.

"It didn't bleed much," he said.

As I held his tooth in my hand, it didn't even look like one.

"It's so little," I said. "This has been in your head for seven years," and he laughed.

"Give it," he said, and he ran home with it in his hand to show somebody, to show to Rachel. He called her 'Ray.'

He would get money from the fairy at night while I made love to his sister in my cell.

"Crippled sister," he said, the day he lost a tooth.

I found her, I thought. I could call her 'Ray,' too.

* * *

And in the sameness in the jail that was a buzz, in those days, the lucky days, she started to look different to me, as she became so familiar. She was a plain beauty, a small, dark haired, pale faced girl. She had a mouth that looked carved out, shaped by a strange language. I wanted to write a letter to someone about her, that she, in her unnoticedness was 'terrifyingly beautiful.' I would wait and get a reply that would say, "You must be completely transformed!"

She was like a schoolgirl, a girl who rode a bus, the right way, always watching out the window, seeing the way she did, and thinking in that same language that shaped her mind like it did her mouth. She talked to herself, in her mouth, little sounds, even when she was with me.

I licked her face in the nights I had with her alone. She was a woman; I knew her insides.

Once, at the fence, I got my hand through. She wore a dress. She felt drawn; she got up as close as she could, her knees and thighs pressed against the fence, pushing into it, leaving marks on her. She had her legs apart halfway. Her body got against it. She held her white side-face to it, and her hair acted as a thin pillow. It was strandy, and blowing around some, moving slightly into her face with the breezes. I put my hand under her dress, stuck through the fence as much as I could. I could feel her thighs.

She said, "Yes, do that... to me." She held her tongue behind her teeth, her top teeth, with her mouth open some. She watched my hand disappear under and then she watched my face with one eye, then she closed it. I moved up against her; she was little, and it was sweet. I pushed one finger towards her along her inner thigh. She gasped; she pushed closer to the fence - it was becoming clairvoyant, it was a chaperone. I held my finger as close to her as I could. I didn't move it. I was breathing in and out with her.

Her nose and her upper lip, had that little place cut into her there, it was cut so perfectly, like into a pumpkin. Her hair reflected red in the brown. It was newly cut.

"Rachel," I said, "Kim." When I said her smaller name, I moved closer to her. She made a noise. She poured herself onto the wire.

And she said once, "Put it in." She turned to face me full, her forehead balanced on the fence. Her eyes widened and I could feel her tighten herself. "...they're watching us," she said.

"He's watching."

I turned around, pulled away from her, to see. There was someone watching, through a window behind me.

"Why does he let you?"

"I don't know, really. It's strange. He likes you, I know. He said the other night that he didn't care about anything. 'I don't care if I die,' he said. He was standing near my cell door, smoking, and he talked shaky. 'I just don't care,' he said. I was lying there and listened. You were with me, and you were lying there, too, really still."

"You're so funny about me being here with you at night, like it's so real. Lucky for us he doesn't care if I'm here, now, right?" she said.

"They probably should care. But we shouldn't talk about it. We can't jinx it."

"I feel a little different now, since you touched me."

"I know. Did it feel wrong?"

"Well, different, out here, in the outside. But nice... my knees felt like roses, sort of weak."

CHAPTER 19

We put many things through the fence. I thought people in the town, the ones that drove by, must've wanted her to not be there. I never knew if they did or didn't.

We put our mouths to the fence, and our thoughts, always, and fingers, and Rachel's knees pressed that way, but not often. She always wore something I loved to see: her colors, and her body, the some of it that showed out the openings. Her face was against the fence so long, there were marks left there.

"I have to walk around awhile sometimes," she said, "to wait until the lines disappear, before I can go home. They'd know what it was. So I carry a little mirror." She held the mirror in her hand.

Her breasts pushed through the fence some, sometimes. I touched them at her heart. It got warm there, in between her breasts. I could feel people watching, but we just let go, and felt melted, and made of tiny parts.

I touched her teeth. The waist of her shirt sometimes pulled up, or her shirt pulled out of her skirt, and I could see her waist, and once her ribs. I loved her there.

She didn't seem to have many seizures anymore. "Maybe they were faked," she told me, "but I don't think so." I felt her quake once, when I was inside of her.

"Next time I'll wear a circle, made out a ribbon, a ribbon

around my waist, out of velvet," she told me. It would frame her, wrapped, below her rib bones that showed through her thinness. We wondered about the baby, and about us, who we, and it might be.

Then she said, and her forearms across her chest were thin and Catholic, "Just once a day please say, Jesus and Mary, I love You, Have Mercy on Us and the whole world."

"Yes, I'll say the little prayer..."

We began to write notes, rolled and passed through the fence, and held by me, sometimes for hours, then to read again at night. I held them and slept with them, to see where they'd be in the morning. I never found some of them again.

She used to walk by my house sometimes and sit on the carpenter's brick, the kind with the two big hand-holes in it. She sat on the solid, smooth side, out in the side yard under the tree that turned purple in the springtime.

She wrote me about it. "I went there again today. No – I don't want to go inside, not yet. I don't know why. Maybe the you now wasn't the you then – and it'll scare me. You said you had papers, and things stacked up. I looked in and saw them that way.

"Yesterday, because I was looking in, a pile of books fell over onto the floor. Were there pressed little flowers, rose petals between the pages? It looks real old in there.

"You look young to me. So young, like a boy."

Next day: "I went there again. There's no one ever around. The grass is grown pretty high. I had a small seizure, I fell against the wall under the windows, and clenched my teeth hard, and laid down there for awhile. It was soft, it was safe. The green, tall grass, and me shaking in it. What would someone think? Our baby was shaken too, just an inch or so away from the grass. Maybe green light came in its window, into its world. A world – inside me."

I prayed the little prayer. I began to think that maybe there could be a God, and He could have come here and been a man, a good man, and loved everyone, even the men who killed him. He loved them while they were killing him, and he forgave them because they didn't know what they were doing...

And I hoped, I expected Him to finally, to eventually be there when it was right, to take me out of here, to take me home, to let me see Shiny, and the baby.

I knew what the baby probably was.

Rachel said: "... I was crying because it felt so good to love, and I didn't know why, or how all this was happening to me and to us. I was in the yard at your house, at the brick – I like to sit there, by the tree, and then I had a shake, and I was crying and trying to see, I don't know why, I just felt that I had to keep my eyes open, and I was falling and I was seeing through a blur and I felt it – I felt something move inside of me. Carl. *It's real*, I thought, *our baby is real*. We've made a child out of our thinking and wanting and talking and writing even just a little and I felt the hand like you said, on my stomach, and the movement inside me. I cried and I shook and I finally closed my eyes. And there were gestures, like a story in my head..."

We talked at the fence.

She said, "I feel the warmth of the hand there on me a lot, at night in my sleep. It's the hands of a story, trying to tell me, maybe to warn, maybe to explain, and maybe –"

Written in her small hand: 'I was in prison and you came to visit me...'

And Rachel, dear Kim, went back every day to the stone in the yard at my small house. There was a notice on the door. She read it. It was a Police notice about the house being a part of a Court order or action, or something, she told me.

"I stood on the step and read it. It was as tall up as me. I feel like I need to protect myself; I felt like that very much when I was reading that.

"When I turned around I saw a man I've dreamed about. He was so familiar, he had that feeling to him, and he came up to me. He asked me if I lived here. I told him no. I crossed my arms in front of me, over the baby. He asked me if I knew who did, and I said yes.

"'What's your name?' he asked me, and I told him, and I felt at each word I said, that I was going to cry, closer and closer. He said he saw me here before, a few times, and he asked why I came here. I told him I was a friend of the man who lived here.

"'Once, he lived here?' he asked me. I said yes. He said he saw me lying down in the grass, crying, and was I okay? I said that I wasn't crying, really, and then I felt there were tears on my face, and I was really crying and pretty hard, and I said I wasn't crying that day, but that I was sick."

"'Are you going to have a child?' he asked me, and I said yes I was, and I was away from my body it felt like then, and I was really crying, Carl – and I sort of collapsed, into him, and he held me up by my arms, under my arms. I let myself rest against him for a minute, but then I felt I needed to pull away and be careful. He said not to worry, and that it would be alright, probably.

"I asked him who he was, and he said he knew my parents. Don't, please don't tell them, I said, and he smiled and said he wouldn't.

"'They'll find out soon enough, won't they?' he said. He stood in the dirt in front of your house, in the alley way. We were there for just a little while. He said not to worry, but to just go on ahead, and that it was alright to be afraid, that it didn't matter. He said goodbye to me and that maybe he'd see me again somewhere. I watched him walk away. At the end of the alley he turned and waved at me."

Then for a few days, it was like before, sweet, and mild and a nice weather and nothing like the strangeness that was happening to us.

Many times she was out there waiting. She stood away from the pen, and then she'd see me. I knew sometime I would just walk out through the fence and have her with me.

When she left, sometimes she went back to the same spot she'd stood in and waited. I watched her there, feeling the stretch of us. She looked down at the ground after awhile of me looking. Sometimes she held the sides of her pants, or her dress, clenched in small fists. She would turn around and let me be. She walked away in a slow way, or she'd run, quickly, fast, and go away to be out there, where I was shut out of, from other people.

We were in the middle of something. A pack of dogs went by one day, like a gang. They looked at us. Rachel was on their side of the fence. She turned to me; she pulled herself as close as she could – her face, its side, pressed so hard against it, and I was scared, very afraid for her.

CHAPTER 20

Rachel asked me to remind her, what it was like for us in our nights together.

I said it was like hot candy in your mouth, and then cool.

"Sometimes it could get so hot in the mouth, so hot it would heat your whole self up with pin pricks and damage.

"Remember making tinfoil Valentines boxes when you were little, and with those red hearts and stuff on it. It's like that sometimes, after we're together, after the heat, like that, to carry under your arm."

She said, "It's fun when you tell me. I know I turn bright red."

Rachel said she found a book at the thrift store:

"I never go there. But I did and there was this great book. It's kind of a religious book, by a young girl. I was never a religious person, really, before, but I did love something, something I didn't know what, maybe just some sort of ghost that was around.

"The girl in the book wrote, 'I feel in myself, a sort of revolt at this extraordinary love in my life. It disturbs me... but I'm happy.' I liked that. I saw that man there, too, standing around in the shelves. He didn't see me, I don't think.

"I went into the drugstore, in the back, you know, at the counter and had a milkshake and started to look through the book. The girl in it talks a lot about God, and His Mother in it. She says that God's strength is infinitely greater than our weakness. It's all about accepting His mercy to wipe out our offences. It says we all have a Mother to who we can turn to in every necessity. Pretty neat stuff, I think."

"You're pretty nice to read about all that," I said.

"And you listen to me – no one ever has. It's a small book, with big words. She was a real person, a girl like me, sort of, but luckier, to see God."

"Yeah. I can't say anything to you but yes," I told her. Then we both were hit, at what was possible here, what we were making.

So she said that I should listen and maybe get ready to hear something serious, so I did, I got ready, and what she told me was serious, and tore a hole in my past, a hole in a hole that was already there.

"Well, I called those people," she said. "I had to, I don't know why. They were still there. Amazing…"

"What people?" But I knew. I saw their faces, though I had never seen them. Some picture of a home I always hated, and feared, and loved to think of.

"Shiny's foster home. You said their names once, like you shouldn't of - now don't, please don't get sad about it. I called them, and we talked. I said I was a good friend of yours, and that you needed to know about Shiny, and how she was and everything, and to talk to her."

I knew my face got smaller, but on the same bones. My chest felt buried.

"I haven't talked to them in about twenty years," I said.

"Carl. They told me they didn't call her Shiny – they said she insisted that they did at first. We talked for quite a little while – but that they never called her that, but Elizabeth, her real name, and how she always wrote *Shiny* though. And they said they talked to you a long time ago. They asked how you were. I said you were doing really good.

"They got funny then, and far away. So, where is she, I asked them, and they were quiet. They said, didn't Carl tell you? I said what? And they said that Elizabeth died. That they told you when you called. That she died when she was seventeen. They never heard from you after that, they said, just that one call, after those years of separation. They said they were afraid Elizabeth never fit in.

"Carl, they said that. They said that to me," Rachel cried.

"Don't," I said, "don't do that..."

"They said she missed you, her brother, so much. Then they said, to give you their best. They said they were sorry, they thought you understood.

They said, 'we asked him if he wanted to come and visit where his sister lived, and to see her grave,' but that you said no. Carl, why didn't you tell me that? Didn't you want to?"

"Elizabeth died. But I don't know what it even means...," I said. "Shiny, my sister died, it might be true. Away from me. If she died she died because of me. Her grave? No. I missed her too much. It's true.

"But she's not really dead – I talk to her, all the time." I saw a picture of Shiny, cut out and stuck somewhere in the ground.

"I have to go inside now."

I turned and went inside where I lived. I went down the hall to my cell, and went in and closed the door on that.

'She never fit in,' I thought.

"Shiny," I said, "It was me that named you that, it was me. I never meant to do that stuff to you." I prayed to her. I talked to her: "I don't want you to be dead, I don't. Please, don't be that far away..." and I started to feel her like always, and a warmth, but thinly. I remembered that her body was gone. I felt lost, and I felt sideways.

That old day, right after I called there, for Shiny, I went into a drawer of stuff I kept - with some of her things. I got out one of her shirts she used to wear. It was folded up nice. I wanted to put it on, but it was too small. I stood in the corner, near the closet. I held it close to me; I patted it on its back. It was so small. It was a blue shirt she wore.

"It's okay," I told her. "It's okay, Shiny. It's okay." I said it over and over again. "I'll never see you again." I tried to move around the room with her. But I couldn't. I held her shirt tight to me, close up against me into a corner.

I went into the shape of my mother's death, and I never came back.

'I should have died as a child to have missed all this.' I felt my mouth get red and twisted. I was all hot and wet in me.

"God, she was the most beautiful girl in the world."

* * *

I stayed in my cell for a few days, to sweep up. I heard that I had a visitor. I could imagine that. She may have had a baby-something inside her, too. But it was too strange, it was like a beautiful, mangled wire fence someone had troubled to wrap colored lights around.

She'd come and stand on the pavement, and then she'd wander off. She held paper, and a small mirror. I sat on the edge of my bed and tried not to think.

I saw how it must have been. I saw how Shiny had been, there. In the beginning, wanting just to keep her name. She stayed alone, as I had. I'd had more than one home. She never fit in. She could be loving. She, with her thin wrists, she didn't cut her wrists did she? And with her hands, she could have pet her new people. And at night, or in the day, at anytime alone, behind the new schools, or in the dark, in her mirrors, in her bed, she would try and return to us, who had been taken from her.

I saw her looking like Rachel. I watched her as she ate dinner in her new home, saying separate words like 'please.' Her face would have shown them if they'd ever looked. She only lived for four years more. Her little hands to hold a black telephone, to call me. I would have run away to her. Whatever happened to Shiny? They never let us talk, as they said it was for the best. They murdered her, my little girl, my only love, my heart, my God, all my light.

A young, lonely seventeen, a girl, alone with herself, and in her depth, a fear, and a delicacy, a perfect, haunted, cut-out face. She wandered around her town wearing a long coat. Two bright eyes in the dark. I hugged her, I hugged her goodbye. Her voice, it would never have changed. The little girl I once knew – her shoulder blades pierced into my memory.

The girl I slept with when I was a child. I lived with her as a child in a time when we were innocent, not yet mutes, or damaged people wanting to hide in the shadows of the children they'd been.

I saw the smile on her face, in her school picture. I didn't have any of that with me. I had her watch. I got it out, and I looked at the scratches, made by her, made by Shiny.

What was it Rachel said she read, about what God had said to a young girl? – "...believe in the interest in which I listen to your prayer..."

Could that be? I thought.

I have to get out of here, I knew.

I went out into the hall, where the doors of the cells were all ajar. I saw a cop I recognized. I smelled him, first, as I bumped him.

"Let me out of here," I said. "It's over. It's dumb here."

He pushed me. "You think so?" he said. He was big. "You think you can just go out of here– maybe go away with that odd girl out there, hanging around here everyday. Well, you can't. You'll be here for a long time, Carl. You might be in here forever."

I thought, 'Dear Rachel, she cried on the side yard brick.'

I would walk through these walls. I knew it. I would believe it and then do it. I would walk on the water, too. I would muster it up and I would walk through a wall like it was a child's drawing on a big piece of paper. I'd watched how Shiny used to sit and draw, and I knew it would take all I had.

I was drunk on the perfume of God made possible.

I was pushed back against my door, back into my cement room.

I would walk out of here. At the right moment, and yes, I would take the 'girl' with me.

Back in my corner in the black, with my eyes wide open, there was bright red, like lipstick on an ancient remembered face, then on mine, rudely. It would get all over, on the walls, a scary face, on the bars, a gripped place by hands dipped red, and in the air, a smeared image of the hole I tried to fill up with loving her.

CHAPTER 21

At home, Rachel went through fighting, actual struggling in the wallpapered hallways and rooms. The beds and chairs were perfectly at peace before, the vases, and a kitchen, the rooms where they were, and a little brother who watched from underneath his low cap:

"Pregnant! We read your little note to that man." She told me about the scenes, and her face wore the picture. She shook through the telling it.

She made me think of that other man, and how he held her when she collapsed, him seeing her shaking in the grass.

"You're telling us you're pregnant by a criminal! That's great – epileptic and pregnant – How! Tell us how did this happen? How?!"

"He loves me," she said. "That's how. I love him. I know him."

"You know him! I'm going to know him in jail a lot longer than he's in now. Rape carries a heavy penalty with a young girl –"

"Rape! We never even had sex! Why do you say that to me?"

They stopped, to look at her. In that first moment they knew it was true, they knew what they had here, then they fell from that grace back into a suburban box.

"Do you think we're insane? Your parents? Well, we're not..."

"You think of me as a minor, or a child or something. Why is that, anyway? I'm a person. I'm me. I'm twenty-three years old. I've never done anything; I've just lived here in this house. I've never even come close to having sex with anybody! But I could – I could, and I would!"

The way they moved after that, she said was like a dance, a beautiful dance they hated. And they couldn't make her stop seeing them that way, as they moved around the room.

"My mother said she would die – she would kill herself if I had your child."

Then I knew, what could be, that twice, people could die, by their hands, because of me, because of me and their daughters.

She said, "This thing we're in, this truth has a power, and we have to be able to say it, and it makes everything wonderful, if only just for us. It makes people crazy. We have to run away."

"She can't kill herself, though," I said. "You can't live with it." I saw the small, cold glint of a knife blade, and I saw the knife in someone's once-loved mouth. The quiet times that lead to the blood coming out of the body where it had been held, for a higher purpose.

"I thought you were younger," I told her. "I'm glad. It's funny I didn't know."

"I'm not young," she said. "I've lived though, like I always was. How old are you?"

"Old," I said.

"Do you really believe in the baby?"

"Well, I do, Rachel, I do, I just don't understand how. Are you sure?"

"Of course I am. I feel it everyday. I'll have it checked. They said I have to. Plus, they said not to come down here, anymore, of course. And they're gonna tell the cops, too –

"My mother – she pushed me hard, against the wall, and I had a fit. I felt my eyes go up in my head. I felt embarrassed for the first time in front of them. They stood there and looked at me on the floor. And I thought, 'don't they remember me, who I am? That I was their little girl?'

"I'm getting out of here – soon. I'm gonna walk out. I have to – I hate them, what they do, what they did to you, and now to us."

* * *

Outside, Rachel was coming near. She was crossing the street. Rachel wore a dress. A man watched her from the other side, then turned and kept going. He went down the alleyway by her house. In the day her house was quiet. He walked beside it, and then was gone. His hands and his face matched.

I thought he had touched her with his mind.

She said hello to me.

"Still here, I see," she said.

"Yeah. You, too," I said. She smiled. I would paint little pictures on her teeth, if I was out, little intense figures.

"I'm sorry," she said, "about the other day. I'm sorry I made the call. I just found myself holding the phone and hearing a voice –"

"It's alright. I don't know about her, think about her, as that way -"

"As dead?"

"Yeah, not like that. No one's that. It's a way to be, it's something to be, isn't it? I just feel her around, so that's what I know. All my life she's been there. There's nothing 'dead' about it."

Rachel stood, with her fingers in the places they were used to, her fence routine; now she was a veteran.

"I do, though, worry some – it messes me up. I think of certain details of how she must have felt, how she must've lived her life, that she felt alone, and – she was much, so much too good for that. I guess things happen you never knew would.

You could wake up all messed up some morning, somehow, and it would stay with you, and then become a normal part of you, and then more stuff, till you were eventually a cripple and dragging around the streets, and yet it was just normal to you."

"That's what I am –"

"No, you're not, not at all. You, you are completely beyond reproach."

"You know, most of my life I pretended, I thought I was pretending to be screwed up, and poor, and out of it, and that I could change it anytime, that I was just sort of waiting for the good stuff to drop in on me, like it should, but then it didn't, and things just got worse, and then I believed it– and then I saw myself as I was, and not as I thought I was pretending to be... That was scary.

"I did call for Shiny – that was before, before I went away.

"I was always waiting for her to come back home, and I was lazy. I let myself get messed up – kept waiting, waiting, until I forgot what for even. I kept waking up in the middle of the night with horrible realizations of who I was. I couldn't sleep. The last ten, fifteen years are like a black out.

"Now I've been forced out of it. I've gotten clear. I'm where I was when the dream started, but older. It's hard to believe any of it – and she was so funny sometimes, she wasn't always just like a picture for me, she was funny, and she was smart. She was real. She was my sister. It shouldn't have happened to her, to us.

"We were doing ok, as kids...and it got so screwed up. It was never her fault at all. She was perfect...perfect."

I started to laugh then, or do something; it felt like I had been talking for hours. "... Shiny was always so nice, I keep seeing her hands holding a telephone, if we had talked, even once, just gotten to talk. It shouldn't have happened. It's so hard...to be without her."

I felt my forehead on the fence, hitting it, and also on Rachel's fingers – they were turning red where I was hitting them.

She carried a small hand mirror in her pocket to see her face -

"— see it's like dream stuff, everything I am, see – dreamed up, dreams of my house, and the town, and Cokie – God! That whole time, I have no idea how she must've seen it all. A drunk seen by a child. A nightmare. When I think of her – I know she walks near my house a lot when I'm in there, or asleep – I just – I don't know, I keep thinking about things that are meaningless."

I put my hands up high, grabbed the fence, stretching it.

"It's alright, Carl –isn't it –?"

I thought of that man. "That guy – how was it to see him, ok?"

"Who?" she said.

"That man – you were with, just now, walking with. He was watching you. He was right there. He's the guy you talked to at my house, isn't he?"

She stared at me. "I haven't seen him," she said.

"Rachel, you were just walking with him."

"He wasn't there! You're scaring me! No one was with me – no one's ever with me –" She edged the words out of her mouth; her teeth got in them.

"I thought I saw a man near you – like who you said, but, now it's fading –" I reached up and touched my forehead up above and between my eyes.

"Forget it –"

"What can I say, Carl? I don't know what to do? Try and forget some of it. I came to tell you I went for a test. If they say I'm pregnant, then I have to go live somewhere else. I will have to – and I know that I am."

"I have to get out of here," I said.

"Me too. You're just like me."

"I'll get out, and we'll just do something. We can just go. This is over. We'll just go away, and be gone. No one sees you, no one even notices you in a new place. We're gonna get rid of our memories and leave."

I saw the two of us, walking somewhere together; I held her hand. She was skinny, and would ride around in an ice cream truck. I knew she'd hide in the backyard.

She did make faces – they could've been called funny - they were beautiful, like a movie on her face.

"Look at your face," I said. "It's so great."

One hand flew up near her face.

We would walk far away.

"On the face of things..." she laughed. "Everything is fine - I'll take your memory, and you can have mine."

While she looked on then, I could feel her stomach tighten in a knot. It came untied in her and was starting to fling loose. Her eyes fluttered, her fingers gripped into two fists... She tried to smile at me, and speak. She looked down. "It's not great."

I tried to touch her. I loved her where her legs and her feet turned inward. I wanted to feel it inside me, deeply, her out here in a dress, at a jail, seized – and she talked to me in my own language, about strings, and shadows, and dreams, and children of the past. If she got a piece of my memory it would tear her in two, I thought then.

I got a note from her the next day. She left it off, early in the morning, rolled up and tossed through the fence, with a rubber band around it, a yellow newspaper one, blackened with the print. I put in around my wrist.

"Well – the test said *NO*. But I am. This will just make it so much easier for us to get together, or to go. I'm twenty-four years old in August. On the 19th. I can do what I want to... love and more....R-K.

p.s. See, it must be true, and dear God is protecting us from them who'll never believe in anything. Bye. I dreamt of you last night in that place I told you about. It was about so long, long ago stuff, too –"

It was a note written on a piece of lined paper, in a shaky

hand by a girl I knew, an epileptic girl with a notion inside of her, and now gotten into me, and we were tied up by it, and I knew I would do things because of it, soon. And where would we go, to where we hadn't ever been before?

CHAPTER 22

Joey cut herself in her mouth with a knife to bleed me out of her, the anguish. That had been a night, a night I saw someone slapped through a kitchen window. She had a knife in her mouth, and he knocked her down. I saw her face seeing me as she fell. There was blood on her lips and a small knife flung in the air.

Her baby was upstairs in bed, and I was outside looking through the kitchen window with yellow tape run across it. He tried to push himself into her, on the floor where I could see. It would be his curved, bone-knife he stuck into her in a stricken, hateful night.

I ran into her house, where I was not allowed. I fought her husband. Everybody cried. She hid her face from me. She locked herself in their bedroom. When I finally left, it was the last time I ever got near to her. He held me hard by the arms when I tried reaching out to touch her.

I ran the jail water. The bed was held to the wall by two strong chains. It was metal meshed, the bed. My feet, as I sat on it, touched the floor. I sat in the cell with the other silent things there. They had their own silence. I thought of an empty jar, now lonely, like me, but that emptiness could contain anything. You could put anything you wanted to inside it. The emptiness would hold it, anything, equally. Where did the emptiness go?

Did the emptiness become the stuff you put in it? Was I like an empty jar that was pure, that held things like pictures, and thoughts and ideas and pain, and Shiny and Rachel? I loved them so much. When they were inside me, I was them. I was nothing by myself but emptiness waiting to hold something. So maybe it was what we put in that made us good or bad or hurt or happy, and that empty container was the same in all of us. I liked to think about it because my contending self was the same as Shiny's and Ray's, and so I was with them there forever. I let them love each other as well.

I pictured the other prisoner, an older man – he had the creased, browned look of having been on the road, in and out of jails, and single rooms for years. He wheezed in the night; I heard him. I imagined him filling up his empty jar with his old blood, killing himself, neatly, being one-time neat. I avoided his face.

My hands crossed over my heart. I felt my heartbeat. I heard yellow sounds, they felt stringy, red was the taste in my mouth, from Rachel, and the blue that came down my hall was the angel. Tonight was my last night in jail, for now. I saw myself out somewhere in the weeds.

It was simple: I knew the fence. I knew the space around the fence. I knew both sides of it in this easy jail. I could move from one side through to the other. I imagined the space inside the fence, where it was soft, where it wasn't metal-gray, but clear, empty of color. In the empty place was the freedom where I would go, where the jar had its emptiness.

Then I'd hold her whole hand, and put the flat of my palm on her face. When she shook to come apart, I would hold her. I would see her mouth without wire in front of it.

I thought: what do I think of in order to believe, to prepare myself to walk through a wall? A wall of thick wire, to undraw, to unknow as that one way; a stubborn wall to make it bend and open itself to me. Hate would not, I knew, open that wall for me. I knew I couldn't do anything, *Without You*. I couldn't do anything without You and never have - no one has.'

I got excited. 'You are our life, even if we don't see. I knew then maybe, I'd never been judged.

I remembered being inside my sister – had I been in her, or was it just imagined sadness?

Her hands may have squeezed my sides. "We always wanted this," she said to me, "didn't we – all together in one body – and young – didn't we?"

Not young now, I knew, not young ever.

The thoughts came in, to walk through on: A young Amish girl, I'd seen, in a shoe store. She was behind a curtain, in a used clothing store. She tried on and then stood by a mirror, in red tennis shoes. I saw how they looked on her, her ankles, where her feet disappeared into their red colored cloth.

Red high-tops below a long blue dress. She bent at the waist, leaned way out and stared down at the shoes, at her feet. She almost leaned off-balance. Her hair fell to her chest, long and straight-soft, loosened from a bun she wore tied in the back when she entered the store. I noticed she had very small teeth when she smiled, but not at me.

Red shoes for an Amish girl.

She tied her hair back up, and left the store, barefoot. She carried her regular brown shoes, tied together by their laces, dangling in her hand, dangling down now in my mind, and some of their color coming down off them, like paint dripping down to the ground.

The red shoes stayed in the store, their red coming off in faint smudges on the floor where they sat. And I could feel her hand on me, thin and light, like Shiny's had been, and Teresa's, too.

I thought of the empty jar, its nothingness, and the open mouths of those two girls.

I thought of how the light comes up and overtakes the night, catches up with it, how it vanishes, and that point where they both could exist together, but there never being a stop.

A hole in the water. A hole in my arm, sewed together, come undone again once as a boy. My Dad had looked at it. He covered it with his hand. He left us all, and he died.

A birthday party for a girl.

A hole in the middle of a woman is why.

Cokie's breasts, into my mouth, and disappeared, coming up from her young chest. Her head went back, eased, and her chest pushed up off the floor to me. She liked to lie down on my floor. I tasted a blood taste from inside her. Her chest turned red and swollen some in two places: the wrongness of it all. God, forgive me. She was so lonely.

Those red shoes could just as easily have walked a dirt road home brighter.

She could have prayed in those shoes.

Holes: in my mother's head; she tossed it back and forth on the floor. I tried to stop it with my shirt.

A virgin I helped myself to. I tried to wrap her back up from a loss.

Cokie had words written on her hand, written in pen to try and not forget, scrawled like lace running up her arm.

How the world arrived out of nothingness, out of a shyness.

A pair of shoes to be feared.

I went deeper, into those holes.

Devil made one into many.

I lay there.

Joey said, "Whatever happens – if the worst happens, meet me in heaven will you?

The part in Rachel's hair was dark red.

I was never afraid of Shiny.

I'd rummaged through the trash in an alley looking for a

beer to drink. Someone passed by the entrance to the alley, a couple. They stood and watched me. I used to know them, somewhere in school. I could still feel: I felt ashamed. I turned away and kept rummaging.

At my home, Cokie would be coming there soon. I saw her jump over a white fence. I saw her legs.

And Cokie with a bottle at her mouth all day long, filled up with it. She tasted that way too. She was a little girl that had been in my house.

Rachel was made to be that way by a smallness disease shaken into an endless childhood:

Mercy was the only way out through the fence, for the asking. Some kind of love mixed in with blood. Blood kept coming in my mind, please wear those shoes out of here, please wave at me, the knowing-blood, connecting, where the blood of the body turned into the light of the mind. The little tunnel where that change took place, and it was true that these women were mostly in that switching-place, is what they were by virtue of that place having consumed them, mercifully.

(where i met cokie was at a fair where i sold colored cups to drink out of, kiln- made, we were under a big circus tent, and the people milled, slowly, and ate and watched, and i watched her, she was with her mother who watched too, and maybe because i wore a black leather jacket and had eyes knowing about her as not just a little girl, but damaged, hurt, she let me, and i met her and she was blushed, i gave her a cup to have, a picture on it, of an animal that never ever lived anywhere near here, she held it in her hands, it made her look smaller. she said thank you. she said, you're nice. i said, no, you are. i must have been at least thirty – she must have been at least fourteen maybe older. she ran back to her car that was leaving and so no one inside that car could see, she shot out to me a low, from her waist, wave that went into me, and after that she came to see me and was rummaging in me at night. she knew what i knew: that I could adore her.)

I could walk outside and over to Rachel's place for lunch, and go away with her, anything else being untrue.

CHAPTER 22

Dead people began to arrive. My mother, her face came too close. She was followed close behind by her father, haunted, and sallow, drained out. He looked afraid.

I knew that deformed horse was nearby.

My sister would lead me out of this.

I stuck my head up to see. At night they let me wander out in the hall into the room where the magazines were, and comic books, paperbacks, mostly crime and detective stories, with old, now faded pictures of men, blonde girls, and guns. They let me go into the cage, too, at night, to see the dark and feel the air. This was no jail, it was a test.

I looked outside the cell door, but no one was there. Just the floor to walk on, hard like water.

The jailer was down the hall in the sitting room. He had on shoes I liked: black, laced high, and top-hooked, old, and soft leather. He was reading comics.

I smelled a rose. First the smell, from mind. I looked and saw one on the floor, and then it was gone when I reached to pick it up. I knew I was near the right place. I thought of Bob, that cop, he was in it too, put in by me. I felt him, wherever he was, stirred, maybe shivered.

"..I don't care if I live or die..." was in my head with a missing rose.

I went back in the cell. I smelled the lye, smoked and burnt into my mother's hands.

Shiny – show me your pale colored hand.

They lingered there in my cell. My mother in the ancient background with her father, where they lived. The man she told stories and lies about. My grandfather, a special soul, a drunk, because he could think and project into the world, images onto paper, pretty and not-pretty, and buried with a horse, the one he created that kicked him to death... That was the story we were told.

They cursed him in the place he lived. "Devil," they shouted, along the dirt roads where they lived.

My mother was his daughter. His wife's maiden name was Eugenia Paris, and the descendents must have reached back to the start of time – because here they were. Here I am, still am, here.

He talked to my mother; he was Shiny's grandfather, too. She was scared of him, and almost never said a word at him. He picked her up, high; she looked down from his arms, and I loved her. I was afraid he would throw her high into the air, and that she would go up and disappear into the sky, and never come back down.

He told my mother about himself. And she told me. Now, I told me. About a shiny place where Mary got Jesus from, unmade, then made. I needed to find that place somehow, to fall in there.

'I can pull a real rabbit out of a hat, but I don't need no hat...and so I drink: It's that hard,' grandfather said to Shiny as she squirmed and frowned in his breath.

'We lived out in the country, where it was clean, smoky looking, and a strange clear. I hardly ever knew him to work at anything much. He was a handy man, and a yard man too,' Mom said.

'See – he'd have a picture and push it out of his mind and at that moment – SNAP! A photo. When it came out, it would be the thing he had thought up. He laughed and he wept over it. It knocked him out. There was never anyone like him around where we lived, or anywhere else I knew.

'His head, and his hands and feet would become numb, like needles and pins, he said. He was my father. He had a special room for doing it and a camera with a line and a little rubber ball on it – for snapping pictures from his mind. It wouldn't always be right, but incomplete pictures, in strange colors. I hated the whole damn thing.'

My mother said it ruined her married life. Said she had a helluva time.

'He wore pajamas everyday of his life, under his clothes – sometimes not even under, just around outside, and even to downtown to drink in the bars he went to. He lived with a bottle in his hand, but he really did it, he really could do it – he could create: …"manifest." He'd say.

I remembered the stories, and a cut out, a cleared space in the woods where we sat, me, and Mom, and Shiny – she was only about eight, and Mom told us then about him. We were there visiting some people, I can't even remember who, and the leaves of the trees were purple, and red, and yellow. It was almost cold out, and clean. We were in a clearing out in the middle of the woods, to talk. In the house we slept on feather beds, the best night's sleep I ever got, never since then so soft.

Shiny and I had two beds in the wood-floor room. In the dark we reached out and touched our hands across. I got up and pushed the beds together. It made a push-screech noise on the floor that was above the kitchen. I imagined the people sitting below, sitting in the lit dark, talking with their cups, and a yellow cloth on the table, us above, alone in the all-dark, in our white, pale clothes, caught in a sound pushed together so we could hold hands all night while we slept in the great soft.

Dreamed things, all cluttered, and bright, coming out of our heads and landing on the bedroom floor.

* * *

Sometimes in the night I'd hear a noise and wake, and taste sleep in my mouth, then remember, and feel Shiny in my hand. I'd put my other hand past her, around to her back and pull her close to me and hold her there, and listen to her breathing, and hear it change with what she might dream. I saw her there as something more than my sister.

I wanted to wake her up, too, because she'd taste her mouth and open her eyes, and come out, and never be mad, but wonder, and would always smile, and watch me watching her. I got to do that many times over the years. Sometimes she'd say, "Stop it."

In the clearing, Shiny broke tiny twigs and branches into a little pile.

"I was a little girl like you are now, Elizabeth." My mother called her that sometimes.

I saw Shiny's white face that day, a dark-haired girl, her cheekbones matching the checkerberries up there in the evergreen trees, as well.

I saw her legs when she stood, in the certain way she walked sometimes for me, marched, her dress blown up to reveal her thighs, thin and smooth. I was familiar with her, all of her parts and places.

She had her chicken pox not too long before that time. There were a couple of small marks left on her face to see, whiter than her face color. They'd been in her hair, on her scalp, too. I touched them with my fingers.

Her face, that day in the wind with our mother; Shiny wore a short coat, skinny, pale-legged, and having piled up broken sticks and left them there, not burned, but waiting for her to return.

Rachel and I could go to that place, together, where we had been. The people that lived there – maybe it was Aunt Helen, but she was lost, long ago to me – were probably dead. Someone had a chicken coop. Shiny squatted down to look in, and poke her fingers through. I wanted to rush her, and grab her body, and squeeze her. She was so there, and ready to love me.

* * *

I started to get up from my cot. I thought of Bob, out there. He came into a corner of my mind. Then, later, I knew he was outside in the dark, by the jailhouse, leaning, and thinking: and not caring, like he said about dead or alive, and feeling like it was time, like I did, for me to be gone away. And because he drank, it created a liquid tunnel, from him to know me, and I'd whisper into his deadened ear: come here to let me out.

BOOK 2

CHAPTER 23

Shiny was thirteen. I woke up. There was some bird sounding in my memory of that night: an owl. It was deep dark out. I could see the window square. It had thin white curtains hanging silent. We had two beds in one room. I got up and went to Shiny's bed. I remembered the cool feeling of the floor on my feet. I pulled down her covers; they were part of her, thin, and Shiny-smelling, sweet. It was just something to like.

I got in with her, behind her. I lay into her, breathing for awhile until I was almost sleeping again. She said the next mornings that we might have dreamed the same things. They never collected on the floors at home, though.

Before I was asleep, I moved down the length of her body, my face against her back; it was small, warm, soft, and hard, a living sister, and friendly. I tasted down her t-shirt until her skin came between it and her underpants. And she was stirred. I left my lips there for awhile, and she fell quiet. I moved down and pulled her pants down, down to her knees. I felt the joint lines, behind her knees, where it was a little bit moist; my sister laid on her narrow side.

I put my palms on her thighs, one tucked under her and between the white sheeted bed. I buried my face into her, where she was soft, and deep. I opened my lips on her. She moved. I pushed slightly, easy, my mouth, into her, into between her hips, into that line: it was like a pencil drawn line, a painting of her in my mind. She pushed back at me. I licked her, and up along to the hard place above, where her tailbone was. I kissed her there very hard. She made sounds; she faced out the other way. Her eyes might have opened, seen the wall in its dark shape, the window square, but barely containing slight, quiet reds, and pales, then closed into her self again.

She put a hand behind her, on my head. She let it rest there; I felt it curl, half-closed. She opened it and pushed my head downwards. I licked her where her thighs were together. I moved up a little and put my tongue inside her as deep as it could go. She let a sound out of her throat, louder, the breath shot out, shaped like a long 'ohhh.' I put my tongue in and out of her. I got lost in doing that. She put both hands down behind my head. She turned herself over some so I could get closer in her.

She brought one hand back and put it like a fist between her legs so they would stay apart for me while she lay still. I did that with her for a long time. She was a bigger girl than I thought.

Then I would stop and lay my face against her there. Soon it would be light out, and when I knew that, I went back to her more, and longer and harder, my tongue, my face – I held her stomach, her chest, and her face with my hand.

I pushed my hand against her face and pushing into her from behind her made a tension and a bending, and she cried into my hand and kissed my fingers, and I squeezed her face harder until I couldn't get any closer to her. I tried to, and I could not, so I kept doing it, and I almost really got lost, and harder and harder until I heard us both sounding just the same, one noise, and I had tears on my face and on her back and shoulders, and arms, wet from me and her, and she turned over and we hugged each other until our sounds and our touch and our breath were just exactly the same. She held me to her as tight as she could, twelve years old, and I did too.

I couldn't stand it. We might've died then, the dawn coming up on us, and the wall, and its pictures and the markings of our lives showing in the light. The darkest part of the night held us, and waited until tomorrow night when we would come back to it, and we did it again, and again, and held each other as close as we could in any way that we could find, and figure, moving and making sounds from it, and sometimes, not always, we cried and held on at dawn.

Then we were tired in the days, and our eyes were larger, slower, and wild at each others, back when our mother was so unhappy, and just before our lives were crushed.

Every night for a long time, until Shiny was gone, the room filled up that wild, close secret of us wanting, and waiting until we knew we couldn't anymore.

I had forgotten all of that, and now it came at me. I took it and remembered the feel of her hands on my head and mine that first night on her smaller face, how she cried and kept it there, and quiet and how I broke and we turned and clung to each other so tight we never could have tried at anything any harder our whole lives.

We had to dive into a swimming pond to make us feel back to normal after those nights, and to look at each other outside, but we never did come back. I still felt it that night long, long after when Teresa put my face beneath her shirt, it reminded me of that whole long place we'd been to.

I kissed my sister in her mouth for a whole night I kissed her body, her back, her arms, under them and along their soft insides, and on her sides. I lay my head, *yes she said yes*, which was bigger than hers, on her chest. We were a picture drawn and held above our childhood beds. I kissed her legs and her feet. I tasted all her tastes, in her everywhere, between her, but not entered, never not even once, misled or even lied to myself now, scared at a possible truth, but a memory of that put as far away as it could be and pushing, Shiny just loved and already missed, even during.

She tasted me like I did her, a boy to her; I couldn't be without touching or tasting her, not anymore, and her face, and in her mouth for those hours that stayed dark for us. Come here, she said, come here to me she said in her arms. We jumped in the water down the street behind the Gordon house. We wore shorts, over, and the little shirts we slept in. We jumped, we screamed to each other under water; we got cold, and we held hands. We sat at the water's edge, and we walked home.

In school that day when I saw her, I touched her on her shirt, at the side of her chest; she wore a plaid, soft shirt. She was so quiet, like the inside of a tree far away, and smiled. I wanted to open our shirts and put our skin together. I told her so and she nodded to me up and down, her eyes widened and then squinted at how lost we'd become. 'I want you to kiss my mouth tonight more than you ever have or ever will again – ok?'

She whispered in my ear. We fell in that dark remembrance of what we were, and I did, I waited all day on her. I did nothing at all but have a heart beat and breath, until we went to bed so we could be together. And it turned out that I did kiss her more, and harder than I ever did or would again, because soon, I wouldn't get to ever see her again.

you named me she said, you, Carl, and you love me. what are we? she said why, and how can we be so like this? shiny, I said in her mouth.

you made me she said, you made me who I am.

Our mother came in one night, she held the door open and we stopped. Shiny made a noise; we held our breath and we three stayed there for some time watching the light that framed the door with her, then she turned slowly and left. We could see her, feel her outside the door, standing, waiting, and then leaving us to ourselves, the doorknob turning silent again, and Shiny turned and kissed my mouth, ours, until I got to forget myself again.

Did we leave her, our mother, too alone, was it that? She whispered only to my sister, that night, behind the outlined door: Shiny, Shiny, Shiny Apalaris.

* * *

We worked, hard, at getting closer than ever before. We knew there was a way and we were afraid of it. We put arms and legs and hands around each other, wrapped each other up and put our heads and faces and all of what we were in between places. We pet at places where the light couldn't get through.

protect me she said push here push please! almost screamed almost mad at how

And we memorized each other so that nothing in our lives later would mean anything at all to compare.

Across one corner of the room we now shared – she had her own room before, and now it was left to itself – sometimes she went there to listen to her songs – she had across her corner a white sheet that cut it off and made a soft wall. She pasted pictures on it and the breezes of the room moved Shiny's wall around. There were pictures of that singer she liked so much that sang about never making a fuss over her, and it was me, I did, I made the biggest fuss in my world over her, her with me, in her single bed, ours now, sister to me, and more; she mothered me, playing, best friend of two people wanting so much.

I remembered – and that night, by way of now knowing, I was forgiven even before I was this person, or with my younger sister -there came through the window and I saw it and kept seeing it until I recognized it: a cross, shaped there and waved, in its shadow on Shiny's curtain-wall.

There must've been a full moon brightening. I could see Shiny's face, and her eyes, and the white on her teeth. There were crosses outside.

I remembered them all at once, many of them being clotheslines or telephone poles or sign places where birds landed then flew and me being raised with that initial impression of the cross, it affecting me heartful, and He, me seeing Him nailed there on each one of them, Him making each one of them hold Him, nailed and killed on each one in each eye that saw and knew and tried not to, and even children at play making innocent crosses and fingers that held that way, or shadows crossed, one of them coming in somehow lit from behind, appearing on my sister's wall.

* * *

And there being a near-last time to everything, we became frustrated. "I need you to get closer to me," she said, "Can't you?" And she would grind herself against me and squeeze me and suck on my skin and my tongue, and drink in my mouth, and hold me to her and cry her eyes. She wanted to put everything I was in her mouth. I got scared and I'd get lost in her letting me.

I pushed myself against her, I got between her legs, maybe never going inside her, her being, me being too young, but I held against her there harder and harder. She put her hands there, opened, and hoarse whispered, after a whole night, voice worn, saying, "I want to, I want to - let me." She wrapped her legs around me, then lay down flat, and I pushed into those two hands I'd always known, Shiny, naked, on her back, sweating, and hair wetted, and face below, and sister pleaded, I pushed up and down on her that way.

I held my face to her neck and against her chest, much like my own, and tasted long, and made red by it, and had to be hidden from our own mother. She felt me, I felt me coming up through me all the long way, to come out rushing into her hands. She was never surprised; she even laughed, and held me tighter. She smiled up at me. She rubbed her hands into her skin, her hands on her chest, and where her legs opened, putting a hand there and holding.

She pulled her legs up high and as tight as she could. I wanted to put my mouth there, and so I did, and she held my face and her self and loved me to kiss her and put my opened mouth to her until we couldn't any longer and she held me with her arms and never had enough of what we wanted to have, even if we'd continued until this moment, and I did that again and again, and was at that place, my face and heart where she would have given birth to me if she could have and maybe did.

I held her hair back from her forehead with my hand, and looked at Shiny's face.

I'd seen her naked on her hands and knees, her face with her hair cut and hung down along it, straight and dark against her white skin.

* * *

I saw Shiny in school, sometimes with her mouth open, talking, or looking or just sitting there by herself, not knowing.

I saw her on the street walking like a sister; I walked with her sometimes. I talked to her, for years.

Then I got to see her backed into a corner away from a

blood pool that she didn't want to understand.

I looked hard into Shiny's face when I held her hair back from her forehead with my hand, in our nights.

CHAPTER 24

In someone's dark room was a hand.

"I'm asleep," he thought. "Now, I'm not. Damn, I'm gonna have to. I have to get up and go and do it."

Someone saw himself in his pajamas lying in his bed. His hand turned on the bedside lamp. He knew how he lived alone. He knew he was lonely. He knocked over the glass of water that was there. He didn't have time to clean it up, or even to straighten the glass. He put his pants on and drove his car in his pajama shirt. He parked in the parking lot near the ice cream store, the window darkened until morning when the children would arrive. He turned off the car and walked across the cement to the fence. White-colored cloth shone out from the shirt that he wore.

"Maybe I shouldn't do it," he thought. "Maybe..." and he fumbled with his big bunch of keys. He put the right one into the padlock and slowly turned the little key. This is my last day on the job, he knew.

He started to open the fence door, and as he did, out came Carl Apalaris striding like a wind that blew him from behind. He walked through the door that was opened. He walked with one hand beside and along his face, blocking, so not to see anything but straight ahead. The policeman watched him walk down the street and turn into a yard of darkness, of shadows, and disappear.

CHAPTER 25

I got up and walked out of my cell, left open, into all that vast space. I walked, led, and full of knowing. I remembered the shadow cross. I walked out into the fence area, that door being unexpectedly not locked, not always, but sometimes, and as I approached the locked, thick wire fence, I moved even faster – and it opened before me – and I was outside, out in the dark night, without much more than a sliced moon, and a short breeze to go by.

I felt big! I moved straight out into it and beyond anywhere I had lately been.

I may have seen a hand, did, and didn't plan to, a hand at the door in the fence, at the part that was always kept locked, padlocked. The memories Shiny unlocked were part of that hand, led there, by hers, a smallish one that had my blood in it.

I stopped in the tree shadows, two houses down from Rachel's house. It was bigger than before, now a real house. It was a dark green painted place that held her. I had her mixed up in my mind now with Shiny. And she was like Shiny, a part of her being invisible, alive, but not seen even by doctors who looked, a baby we made by believing. I made this child physical, and Rachel made this child, holy.

I felt too visible out here on the street. I wanted to run home. If I went there, turned the door handle and even moved one item, a quarter on the dresser, a paper laid somewhere, a chair, a dead flower, moved even the door and the air in the place, it would forever change destiny, for everyone. I waited in the shadows watching for the right hole I could slip into.

A loud car went past. I laughed, at the memory of my father, jumping out of his chair in his white boxer shorts, on a hot summer night, and chasing a hot rod down our street, running and swearing. We all laughed at that; Shiny was little, and she was in a little seat and she laughed because we did, and if anyone cried, she did too.

Later we ran together behind the fog machine, breathing in the poison clouds that moved along the Southern streets to kill the insects. We laid and listened, and watched the fog machines roll the streets like space ships in their red-lighted smoke. We heard the locusts sing and beat against the window screens as we fell to sleep and dreams. Later in those beds we fought to love as hard as we could, it all sticking to us.

"We were like cannibals," I said out loud. I wanted to consume my sister, like we wanted to eat the colored lights off the Christmas trees set up in the living room, liking them so much. Like everyone else, we stuck the angels at the top of the tree. The lights reflected off the cold white table top outside on the patio, even through the window. They ran through the glass to get stuck there on it, the red and green ones the most.

"There are angels," Shiny said, "cause I've met them when I'm sleeping but not completely asleep – and people who follow them around, even though they tell them not to – the angels, they tell them not to, but they do. Who are they?" she asked me. "Dead people?"

"Did you ever see Grandfather there?"

"No," she said, "But lots of animals, and once I saw me, but me looking beautiful, and older," and she looked back at me and was so nice, nicer than anyone could ever be...

In the dark, I backed into some bushes, and got down against the side of a house. I didn't really care. There were no lights on, there was quiet, and a slow, easy breeze through the calla lily leaves. I adored them.

I thought about Rachel, things she had said.

"My mom says it's calf-love. I didn't tell her your age, or she'd been really mad – she just thinks I visited you a very few times – not everyday. She works. And my Dad doesn't even want to hear about it. He said he talked to your cop friend, that Bob man, and that Bob wanted you to be let out, because you hadn't really done that much. My dad says that Bob's shaky – that he's a suicide type – he said.

"Bob told him you were twenty years older than me. He told Mom - then I said it wasn't either just 'calf-love' – but real, and good, and kind, and she got strange when I said we were going to have a baby soon. That's when it started to get really hot – I'm talking a lot, huh?"

"Go on," I said, "please - go on, don't think that."

"They said they'd tie me in the house if they had to, and I thought about if they really did that, and imagined being tied to a rope outside and miserable and what if I lost the baby out there. I saw myself squatting down and the baby coming out, too soon, much too soon and lying down its new head and body in the grass out in the yard, and what if you were out, in here and could watch but not do anything. If he came out like that, with me tied up, I'd just hold him until the folks got home and cut me loose and take him inside. I'd have to leave the cord attached to him until they got home. Just sitting in the yard with my baby.

"Even if he were born too young, he'd be okay, cause he has a purpose to come here – any child born like he's gonna be – through only the thoughts and wishes of his parents – he would be so full of good inside, that it'd be hard to die of anything.

"I'd lie down with him in the backyard, in a big cardboard

box, the refrigerator box that's out there, and just rest – in a box and we could watch the stars at night in it. It doesn't seem like it could be real, but it is. I know it is more than anything else I could know, cause it's inside me – and I know, and it's too late to not have it happen. It must've happened in an instant. I think I remember when, just when I first felt it…one night.

From the cage, I'd watched her talk, and felt close, and far away. I knew that what would or could happen couldn't ever be that strange anyway, so I just let it all be. It was just voices.

"In a refrigerator box, huh," I smiled.

I'd remembered then, that time when she pressed herself against the fence. She pushed from her back to get that close. She sat half-way down. I loved how she pulled her dress way up on her thighs, the bridge it made across her legs… And how her legs bent at her knees, beautiful, and white, against the cyclone fence that made lines that would go away on her short walk home.

And if she went anywhere, and sat down on her behind, on a flat surface, with her legs apart and stuck straight out, in a dress with shoes and socks on, and with a certain tilt to her head: That would end the world as we know it, and is how I felt about her, a girl, downtown, sitting on the cement with the wind blowing on her, a girl who came to visit me.

* * *

From where I was I couldn't see Rachel's whole house, just the front edge of it sticking out. I liked sitting where I was. It felt good, and cooled. I sat deep in the leaves and shadows. I heard a short, falling noise, then I heard steps on the ground coming after it, then a new shadow of someone, small and creeped over, like a girl. It moved into the bushes by the house-side facing me, across a thin yard. There wasn't much light but I knew who it was. It scared me: now I would be a person to her without a fence to look through at.

"Psssst..." she said, across.

"Psssst," I did it too.

She got straight up and came across the yards. She got on her knees in front of me.

"The fence is gone," she said. "Can I join you in the leaves?"

"Yeah, but we'll have to go on soon... C'mon."

"Calla lily," she said to me. She remarked, a girl in the dark.

"Yeah."

She leaned back like I was, against the house. She had her shoulder against mine. She seemed smaller then, and stronger than I'd thought. She turned. She kissed me on my lips. I tasted a metal taste, then her. She kissed me, and I let myself go in her, and felt the ground underneath me and the night air, and her. It was soft, and it was dear. She still kissed. Her eyes had closed, now opened, and she pulled back and looked.

"Hello," she said. "It's funny, huh?"

I licked my lips a little. I kissed her back. I kissed her face, her cheekbones below her eyes, then her forehead. It was warm, and I felt a very slight indentation there. I kept my lips there a long time. I reached over and held her shoulders. I moved my hands to above her collar bones, for balance, and she was with me, and she let me do those things.

"That cop came over," she said, "and told my parents. I don't know why. But he was nice about it. I think he was trying to make them be okay about you."

"Did he talk to you? How'd he get to your house without me seeing him? I think he let me out."

"I never talked to him. I heard him through the door, in my room. My dad told him I was asleep. Maybe you fell asleep out here, in the dark –"

"No, that couldn't have happened – but, maybe. I was thinking, and I closed my eyes. A lot of stuff could've happened while I was out there – anybody could have passed by

— thousands of people - but I don't think so."

We were walking down the alleyway from her part of town. It stretched between the houses, out between the backyards, all the way across town. There was a whole network of them to hide in. There was a big, white-faced town clock we could see almost from anywhere. It was one o'clock. We could hear our feet on the old road. There was couch grass growing along the middle of the way. Joey's house would loom up soon at us in the dark. I didn't want to see it.

When Joey said goodbye, out in a park, I was okay at first, and then I cried and couldn't stop, and she tried to talk to me, and tell me to stop, and then she cried, and we got scared, and I said, 'What if one of us dies, and the other one doesn't know it? I'm scared of all the time I have ahead of me without you.' I held her face in my hands.

'You love me too much,' she said. She pulled back, ran away to her car and was gone.

"So what'd he say, to your parents?"

"He said he'd let you out of jail."

'Then he did,' I thought. "It's funny, him being there, just then."

"He said he'd let you go cause he felt it was time for it. Just time for it. They said I was asleep, and they all probably looked at my door, and at the bottom of it. I didn't have the light on. I was standing behind it. Then they talked about nothing, and I waited till he was gone. I slipped out the window and ran behind the houses, and saw you. We have to get you some clothes. I saw you easy in the leaves out there..."

"I liked it in there; it was a nice place, in those leaves. They never have to do anything. They're sitting under the moon, now, as we talk."

We turned down the alley, getting to the cross point that

led to my house, and Joey's to the left. I erased it. I could just see mine, how it sat, squat and dark brick, with a long, flat, black tar roof, a shotgun house, covered with vines, and bushes all along it. It had been there all along. There were three south windows that faced us coming towards it.

"I'll stay out here. Can you go in?" I asked Rachel. I wanted her to put her hands into my things, in the rooms, the drawers, her arms disappearing half way in. "I'll show you a hole in the bushes you can crawl through – it's a green tunnel that leads to the backdoor.

"You'll have to be like a child though, to get in."

We stood about one hundred feet away. I put my hand from her lower back up on her shoulder.

"I will," she said. "That's easy." I saw her crawling through the crawl place, her narrow behind lying down and wiggling through in her pants.

"After the tunnel, there'll be a back door. It's almost grown over.

There's a key I left right near the crack in the door – in the bottom, in the doorjamb – you know, where it meets the ground – you'll see it. Now, open the door easy, cause there's lots of stuff in the way. Just push it open and go in.

"Can you get me some pants and shirts and socks and everything. Nothing red, though."

Rachel laughed in her mouth. I told her where everything was. I liked where it all was. I liked the red in her mouth. She would be inside there, and the last time I was, was the day after I'd first ever seen her. When she laughed, her chin gave her a new face.

"When you're in there, I want you to lie down in my bed – just get in and get under the covers and be there for a minute. Close your eyes and just be inside the place – okay?"

She said she would do it. When she started to go, I almost forgot everything, why she even knew me, or liked me. I stood there and felt alone in the world. I whistled quietly, after her a little. I'd asked her to touch an old black jewelry box that had been my mother's. It had some white pearl pictures of Oriental girls on it. Shiny had touched it many times. There were things in it, small pretty things they'd both wore.

I watched Rachel crawl under. I knew she'd never crawl through there twice and stay the same. She pushed herself through, and gone, into a child's world, my world, not ever a big one: One night I begged a ten foot, white statue of Jesus, out at the cemetery, to know why, why was there a stunted, a discolored soul as mine? 'Why, God, isn't it enough to love you? Cause I do,' I told him, the statue. 'Who wouldn't, if they thought of you even a little bit – and always out here waiting for us, in all the weather, every minute of our lives wrecked and ruined, and so wild. Mine feels like it got punctured.

'I was never like I should've been,' I told Him. 'I guess I have to be like you for it to make any difference. I've gotten so narrow,' I told Him.

Sometimes I created a God, a God that it was okay to make up, for a little while, even if it wasn't exactly true, a God that I wanted to imagine. A God who loved me no matter what, and was young, too, and colorful, and laughed and was with me and was God alright, but easy and sort of like me. Sometimes it helped, to do that. The God sense within us all, made into form. A God Cokie would like.

Rachel was in my house. I sat at the telephone pole at the crossed alley ways and watched, and I looked up some, too.

A light went on. I thought of the noise a key might have made in the old lock. It was rusty, but it worked. The key had stayed where I put it, a long time.

I could see her, shadowy, through the loose, wood-slat curtains that hung at odd angles. Then I didn't for awhile.

I heard her scream a long scream.

I thought of the empty jar, and the blood-jar from the

older, sinewy man still in jail.

I stayed where I was.

She stopped. She would be lying down. I lay down in the alley to look up at the stars. "I'm back," I told them. I thought about that word, 'puncture,' about putting a point of a knife into anything and watching the air come out until there was nothing left. I'd said it to God.

Her hands got in my drawers, in my closet, along the table, and dresser top, where I never thought other hands would be. She gathered what I needed. When she came out she'd wear a different face. I knew why she screamed.

I could have just walked away, abandoned her, and the idea of the baby made that way, put a big gap between us. I lay still on the gravel, and waited.

Rachel crawled out with my things in her hands.

"I liked pushing along the ground on my chest and my legs," she said. "It was fun."

"Yeah," I said. Rachel found sixty dollars, now in her shirt pocket. I put my hand there and felt her breast. It was small. I liked it very much.

I wished Cokie was out there waiting in the dark, waiting nights for me to come home, her as an uphill, country beauty. Waiting at odd angles. She was like a picture my grandfather would've made. She sat in a cardboard box of old letters, and books and stuff. She sat in them, and laughed. She'd cried, too, sitting other places. She was lying down with me, and she'd jumped crazy around the place. Holding her, my arms came around her to where my hands would touch her sides. Her lungs, when they heaved, were small.

I thought of her blood, close under her skin, how it would look, out on her chest or on her face, if it ever came out, or lined all down her legs, if all of it came out of her at once.

If she'd been there, she'd come up to us, then stand back

and wait and see what. The night was cool out, easy to stand in and wait. Then Rachel would reach out to her and touch her hand or her wrist where her smallest bones were, or her neck, at her collar. I liked that place.

Later they'd hug each other, and kiss, even on the mouth. I could see them, their arms wrapped around. It'd be like jelly was in their mouths, so much, some of it would run out. And they could laugh in it, nine times.

The three of us: someday we'd notice a girl in a blue coat. To put our hands along.

We'd find a pencil poem on the ground: About a red animal. About warm. About a house.

We pulled off our sweaters in the cold; we looked so white.

Like eggs, the white, the underside of our three mouths together. Yes we kissed each other, all at once, all of us, and tasted what we'd said inside.

I'd like to see a red colored cloth, blowing, tied somewhere. "Did everyone hate us?"

Cokie wasn't there. She would be at home in her bed, lying down parallel to the boards that made her wood floor, and her in between the walls that surrounded her, half-prettied, decorated some, but not enough, not caring, never any of these things: house, walls, floor, prettiness, bed, wood, and people – not there for her happiness, but her with an undertook darkness, always with a stone serious face, even when she broke it laughing, or when she took a fall.

"Everyone looks at Cokie..." *what do you mean, spoiled? what have you spoiled in me?* She laughed from her throat. *it hurts me* I kissed her on the stomach. She lifted her shirt. After a while she'd come over and walk in my house and take off her shirt, without any words, then sit down and look at my face. She sat on my lap, straddling my legs, to face me close up. I watched her in my house; sometimes she stood. She wore long pants, without a shirt, her hair hanging down not that far.

And from her back, and almost from her front, certainly through a window, she could have been anyone. For a short time she drew triangles, from a school thing. She wanted to draw them on my walls. She held her fingers together, in triangles, around her breasts.

Cokie said, "After the hurricanes where we used to live, we'd find baby chicks blown out of their nests. We rode them around and around on the record player.....

"We have a disease," she said, and I held her up, off the floor...

"I want to see you, all of you at once, both sides, front and back," I said.

"Inside too," she added

"Don't treat me like a child," she laughed, and she cut her eyes.

CHAPTER 26

Rachel and I moved together towards the big clock. I had on my old clothes, new to this night. We had nowhere to go. So we held hands.

"We should probably stay off the streets," I said. But I felt a joy. We walked on.

"Yeah, I think so," said Rachel. "We both slipped out. Maybe nobody knows yet. I bet my parents don't."

"Would they call the police?"

"I don't know. They might call Bob, and have him check out where you might be. He told them he was quitting though, that tonight was his 'final act of being a cop.'"

"His face was funny, wasn't it?" she said. "Hard to see, in a way."

"Yeah," I said. "Sort of. They don't check on me too regularly, anymore. They assume I'm in for the night, of course. The jailer usually sleeps. It's not like a real jail. But if some cop sees me out on the street, just floating around – with you – you know, I mean, that'd be it."

"They all know about us, huh?"

"Yeah. It's a small town. I used to always like that."

"I might miss going there, to the jail everyday," she said.

"The whole town probably knows about us, too. I never thought of the town very much before, if anyone knew me, or ever noticed me around. I see the same people around but I never imagined that they see me all the time. But I guess they do though –" I said.

"Hardly anyone knows me," said Rachel. "I'm pretty invisible. They don't enjoy seeing me..."

We walked in the alleys in the biggest shadows we could find. I thought about what I had thought about so I could walk out of jail. "I'm no different now," I said. "I thought maybe I would be." I thought about the Amish girl.

"We could walk the dirt roads out of town. We could hide when we saw cars – soon we'd be away—" she said.

"We could, it'd be pretty rough. I don't know. I just want to be with you. It felt like it was time. I know it was, for some reason.

"I know a little place just for now, we can rest in, till we can decide." A straight line to walk to it, crooked to go by, where a ghost of me lived.

"I thought about you coming to my house, and living with me for years, in my room," Rachel laughed, "but – I guess not. It would be really insane – and then when my parents died, or when I got a lot older, we could use the rest of the house."

We got near downtown. It was just a few blocks, in a square. There was a park in the middle, with a statue and with flags all the time blowing around. Hot rods circled the square on Friday nights, and Saturday nights it was pretty quiet.

Sometimes I went there late at night, to the center of the square and sat, in the exact center of town. I sat alone and hated myself.

We ran across the deserted streets. We got to an alley between some buildings. There were a few lights on above us, rooms for renters. The people up there, their weight on the floor, were lost. We were down below.

"... but not all of them," she said.

"No."

"Angels, some of them..."

"Yeah. Maybe we should have hit the fields," I said.

"We still can. We can stop here for awhile and wait and see."

"Look!" I said, and her hand was small in mine.

"What!" She leaned in, sharp, against me. She had chills running through her. Like cold straps.

"Cop car," I said. It came down the slow street, and rolled by.

"I'm glad he didn't turn in –" she said.

"Yeah – c'mon." We walked deeper into the alley. "There's a tunnel up here. I used to go there. Behind an abandoned building."

I touched my chest. I pretended to have on a silver locket with little pictures of Shiny, and Jesus, and Rachel in it. We kept walking. I thought about a chair falling through a window. It was an old, wooden one, like the one I threw through the window at Joey's house so long ago.

"Did you hear something? Like a crash, Rachel? Just then –"

"Huh? No, nothing, just the air. Stuff in my mind –"

It was the sound of blood pouring through our heads.

The sound of it draining out a little bullet-hole.

* * *

Shiny and I sat down on the soft cement, soft like summer curbs at night, or even in the blaze of afternoon. Way back, we wore small, printed shirts; we rolled the sleeves, Shiny and I wore the same kind of clothes, and I got short, summer hair-cuts. We got sun-glasses, and our fingers played in the hot grass, cooled at night, and greener in the dark.

There was a presence and the sound now, not of a crash, but a softly falling chair onto a wooden floor.

"I don't hear much of anything," Rachel said. "Not a chair, not any people - maybe just that light bulb buzzing over there. Maybe they're just sounding for you."

She scooted closer to me. There was something opening here that had nothing to do with her. She turned her face, and her mouth was open to me. I pulled her up very close, chest to chest. My lips grazed her cheek. I held to her. She was more like me than anyone, now.

I heard, from above us, "You – sometimes —" then it was blacked out with loud music – "– hate you," and sobs, like they didn't want to hate, and then sudden silence. We shifted ourselves, and our blood ran next to each other's.

"You heard that, didn't you?"

"Yeah, that," and she sat nearer.

"Kiss me again," she said, "so I won't shake. I'm always on the edge of that – and if I do while you're kissing me, I like it. It's small disease – I don't have it bad. Small mal, I call it, and it's made me stay small, sort of, hasn't it?"

There was something big in the way. I wanted to look at what it was, and there was the chair that kept falling over in my mind.

It was the shape, beckoning me, to a challenge of itself made into a form with sound, a sound of falling down.

Rachel said, "I feel the baby move in me when we get deep, and touch."

And that's when I felt the same loose piece happen, shaped for me.

"In a way, we're strangers," she said. "Cause we don't have the fence."

"If we wanted to, we could unthink the baby," she said.

"We'll just do what we're going to do," I said. "C'mon, I want to go inside here."

Rachel followed me up the stairs. A wind blew up the staircase behind us.

"I used to come here," I said, "but now it looks a lot different, like they added floors – but they wouldn't do that, not to an old building. I used to sit back here and drink, and watch the cats. After awhile, they never noticed me. I talked to them. It's an easy life, like that.

"I like that you're here now, with me."

The cement tunnel ran along the backside of the building. I knew that Rachel's skin looked sort of red, but it was mainly so white, and her hands; and her, walking, and straps inside her that held her up inside. We went up the long stairs. It used to be an old hotel. There was some whisper in me.

At the top of the stairs was a long hallway and doors cutting out off of it. Two doors down, a door was ajar; it gaped at us half-open. There was once a long line of old, browned, used Christmas trees lining the long hallway, making it hard to walk through, some of them still having tinsel stuck on.

From inside the door came the sound of a chair being overturned. When I looked inside, I saw a woman hanging by her neck from a rope.

Rachel made a noise like being hit in the stomach.

"Grab her!" I yelled. "Lift her up –" There was a blonde woman hanging from a thin rope.

It was a dim room; there was the chair, laid over on its quiet, horrible side, kicked over by someone. Her feet were at my waist level; the rope was up, wrapped around a pipe that ran across the ceiling the length of the room.

"She's dead!" said Rachel.

I lifted her up so the rope would slack. I felt her life.

It felt like broken teeth in the place, rough in your mouth. There was sad in there, too.

I lifted the woman, and held her. She moaned, and choked. I saw her eyes bugged out. A woman hung….

"Rachel! Get a knife or something, and cut her down. I'll hold her. Stand up on the chair." The woman's hands hung limp, but curled, and she was half conscious inside my grip.

When I said that about the chair – at that very word – I saw the red glow of a cigarette get brighter in the other room, in a kitchen. Someone was smoking, taking drags. It may have lit up their lips, slightly, but it wasn't clear. I couldn't see who it was.

Rachel ran in there and went through a drawer. She got a long knife. She made a scared noise, surprised when she saw a man, smoking in the chair. He was watching a girl carrying a knife.

She stumbled out into the room, got the chair up and stood so her own stomach was up against the woman's. She cut at the rope. She sawed it until it cut through, and the weight came down on me. Rachel strained, making her noises, almost crying, and then I fell down, the blonde-haired woman on top of me.

Rachel got down and worked at the rope with her fingers. It was yanked tight around the woman's neck; she was still being hanged. We might've walked on by, her being dead now, and the watcher still sitting in the kitchen at his cigarettes. But I'd heard, "I hate you," maybe said by her, and that chair falling. The cigarette sucked, brighter, on and off.

"Lay her down." Rachel had the rope loosed. Now the woman was coughing and racking and doubling up, red-faced. She was spitting out on the floor. The rope was still around her neck. Rachel had her hand in between it and the woman's neck.

"Hey!" I said. "You," – at the kitchen, "What's going on? Why didn't you help her? Huh?"

A man got up. I thought he would kick me in the side. He turned on a little kitchen lamp on the table. What I saw first was his hand, then all one side of him. The smoke was in his mouth, a short cigarette held by his lips. He was tall, thin, torn. He came and stood in between the two rooms in the door way. He let the smoke out of his mouth.

"She gonna live all right?"

"I don't know. Hell, I guess so –"

"She's done it before. Never seems to work how she plans it. I don't know why. She's an abortionist, is probably why."

"Well," I said. Rachel had a pillow from somewhere, under the woman's head. The woman looked up at her. Her hands fluttered in the air. I thought about how there was a knot around her neck. It was a simple knot tied that way to kill.

"That's why she did this?" asked Rachel. Her voice shook.

"She had some trouble with it, lately –" said the man. "Something bad –"

Rachel made a face. "Oh," she said. Her eyes squinted. "Oh, wait..." I heard her say. She sat with her hands run up to her head. "Ohh," she said again. I saw her eyes go up. Then her hands at her face twisted in, her fists at her cheekbones under her eyes. Then she lay out on the floor on her back, shaking, then onto her side. She curled up in herself and was coming apart.

I moved over and lay down by her. She cried out in it. I heard her shoes beat the floor. Her teeth were clenched, her head going back.

I held her as close as I could. I felt her trembling and held on. It made me want to shake too. Then I did. It got in me and shook me almost into pieces. My head banged on the floor until I saw lights. I heard the sound as if from far away. My mouth stayed open and my tongue rolled back and forth, bleeding.

Deep inside, under and behind my heart came a punch, outward, a hit, and my face turned like hers, cramped, and clenched. Before I blacked out, I smelled something – something I hated, something different, but intensely familiar. I heard someone say, "Jesus!"

When I came back, I was in a peaceful place, like with Rachel in the jail-nights, her tossing all over and me quietly inside her. My mouth and head were hot, needles and pins, and a cold sweat was on me. My hair was soaked.

"It happens in a flash," I heard Rachel say to me. Her lip was bleeding too. She touched it with her finger. Her eyes were wet.

"Sometimes I get soaked in one second. I hate it in a way – but it leaves me so still, so drained, I guess."

"What's in there trying to get out?" It was the man that asked. "Wow," he said. "You two are something – what were you doing?"

"Nothing," said Rachel. I looked at her. I took deep breathes for awhile. I sat in the middle of the floor under the place where the rope hung down, cut in two.

"Sit on the couch," he said. "You need some water or something? It's all I got."

"Okay," I said. "Yeah." I sat by Rachel on the couch. I leaned my arms on my thighs and held my head down. Then someone was crying, until I shook, as it came out of me. Rachel, or someone, had a hand on my back. It felt far away, it was so light and small.

I was aware of the woman on the floor. She coughed, but not too much anymore. She lay with her eyes closed. Her hair was covering most of her face. The man sat in the kitchen again. He was older than me. He must've lit another cigarette. I smelled it. I remembered the other smell. It was old.

"It's okay," said Rachel. "It's all right." I couldn't see very well, and I didn't want to. The inside of me felt crushed.

"It's okay," she said.

I lay down on the couch with Rachel, for a minute. I thought about my shoes being on. She was lying against me, fitting in me, where we curved. The woman was on the floor, the man was in the kitchen. He said a few things, but not things meant for anybody to really hear. He sat back down in his kitchen chair. The light was turned off and it was dark again. I fell asleep with Rachel.

CHAPTER 27

When I woke up, I knew where I was. It was still dark out. Rachel had her eyes closed, her face up close to me. My insides felt quiet, but like a separate animal. I heard the man talking in the kitchen.

"I wish I could smell a peach, or something. A ripe peach..."

"You can't smell a peach in here," said the woman, spoken with a raspy voice. They sounded like they were down some, on the floor, lying down on the kitchen floor. I turned around so I could try and see them.

I felt Rachel up against my back.

I could see their legs by the lamp, back on. Someone was smoking. He was lying on top of her, on the floor. They had on their clothes, but I saw their shoes were off. I looked back up, to see the rope still there.

"You only slept a half-hour," said the man. He paused. "My name's Gus. There are very few people named that anymore. I bet not one boy is named that now – a newborn boy or girl that is – anywhere in the world. They'd only name a person that in the U.S., anyway – right? Maybe in England, they would though, huh? I don't know about names over there. Do you?"

He was talking to me. "No, I don't know," I said. "What're you doing in there?"

"Nothing. What we always do." He was quiet for awhile.

"My name's Kit," I heard the woman say.

There were rustling sounds, clothes noises. I knew the woman was lying on her front. Maybe he had his hands around her neck. I imagined a short cigarette in his mouth. It could've been burning her hair in the back. I was searching for the smell of it. Then she made a noise in her throat, in her mouth, like a balloon, a child's balloon, blown up too tight – being rubbed.

Then the man was laughing over her. "I took it all out of her," he said. "All of her life, a long time ago." He laughed short. I saw how her legs were drawn up, where I couldn't see them anymore. I imagined them bent at the knees, up under her, crushed under her chest, drawn up and her made wide open to him. Her hands would be at her knees, holding them.

"I hate this," I said. "I slept here." I turned to Rachel. "Did you sleep – at all – even for a minute?"

"No," she said, "I never wanted to."

"Good, nothing could get to you," I told her. "We gotta get out of here now -"

"Wait," said the man. "Guess what –?" Rachel and the woman should've cried when he said that, but Rachel was leaving, and the woman didn't know how.

"What?" I said.

"I did," he said. "I got in her, while you was asleep. From way over here." And he laughed some more, still on top of the woman.

I went into the kitchen and saw them on the floor. I was right. She was drawn up, thickened in her middle, over her legs, for him. She had her pants off, laid there by her face. He might've been inside her. Now he laid heavy on her.

I picked the lamp up, off the table, and smashed it across his back, and the room went dark. I held its short base and smashed it down into the middle of his back over and over again. Then I dropped it down.

He yelled at us as we reached the hall. His words broke

some in his mouth. "I've seen you before," he yelled, in a kitchen-voice with blood in it, hurt now like Kit was. "Out in the alley, when you didn't know I was watching. You played in the cats. You and me, together; I saw you.

"I mowed your lawn when you was a boy. I knowed your whole life – and that sister you threw away."

I looked back; I could barely see him from the open door. His hair was down in his face, down at his chin, in long pieces. His mouth was shaking. I could hear him spit. He laid there by the woman and yelled, in his sock-feet, at us.

"Now you got this one. You think no one ever sees you – but you're wrong. Everybody knows all about you and that life you live out there in a shack, and gone crazy with a little girl! You're the one oughta be hung!

"Girl – what're you doing with a man like that for?"

Rachel ran down the hall.

I thought to rush back in that kitchen-hell and beat him with the lamp and the chair, and with the whole kitchen table, his face, and his long hair flying against the wall.

I yelled, "You hung that woman – and you never mowed my lawn, or ever seen me before. You lie!"

"You fucked your sister and you been down in the cups ever since. Don't come in here accusing me of anything – this is my wife!"

Rachel was back, and had me then with her hand on my arm, pulling me into the hall, away– "C'mon – c'mon, don't do this —"

"I hate that guy," I said.

"No! Stop being like that. Didn't you see his face? It'll be you then. I want you to be different- cause you're special."

"I'm not," I said. "I'm just a guy. I broke out of jail. I saw you in an old, dumpy cafe –"

Rachel screamed.

"No! You walked out of that place, special. You have to be,

if – if we're gonna do this thing. You have to be, you have to be, you have to be..."

"I'm not that, at all," I said. "I'm not."

"You are. It's too late –" Out in the hall, her mouth, and her words - she talked at me with her hands: "I need you," she said. She twisted around in a dead hallway.

Her mouth began to move almost in slow motion.

"All you have to do is believe in good," she said. I could see some colors on her lips, I thought from where she bit herself. "It's all you have to do – and then everything will be ok." The colors came out of her mouth.

"I've done horrible stuff," I said to her. "I just hit that guy. I wanted to hurt him." I thought back to him like in quicksand. "We gotta get out of here," I said.

"It doesn't matter what you've done - you saved his wife didn't you? From death. And even if you didn't, it's okay – And whether you did whatever you did to Shiny—"

"I didn't —"

"Okay, whether you did or not – stop blaming yourself – you were just a person. I want you to be with me. We made a child, somehow – I know we did. That's special – isn't it?"

I hit my head against the wall. I was coming loose.

The plaster fell behind its green paint. It was like a Mexican-painted, slick glossy horse I'd seen, with gaudy-pretty on it. I hit my head at it.

"That bastard," I said. "He'd like to get to you and take away the baby," I said. "I know it. You have to watch out for him –"

"You can see the world as a good place," she said. That's when I felt the children. They ran down the hall. They stampeded. They rushed around me. They surrounded, and grabbed me; they kissed at me, against the wall, my hands, my sides, my legs. I could feel the touch of little mouths all on me.

Some of them kneeled down and kissed my legs. They didn't say anything, only breathed the excited sounds of hurry.

They pet me, with their small hands. Some buried their heads into me. I felt a burning, like a small brand burned into a shape into me, at the base of my spine. I smelled it. (*and I will have a new name*) One child held the brand up, another lifted my shirt— they all crowded around: they yelled, soundless. Then they were gone. I heard them running back down the hall to the long stairs we'd climbed.

"Could there be beings, like angels down in this world?" I asked Rachel.

"Yes," she said. "I hope so – gardens of them, housefuls. This place, this hotel – it could be filled with bright blue ones, angels, hotelfulls of them. Maybe we just don't see them.

"Even God could be down at the end of the hall waiting, if He wanted us to come to Him – it could be that way. This could be heaven; it could be seen that way –"

"But, it isn't," I said. "It seems like hell, more –"

Things jumped into my mind, to touch me, touch me where it feels so weird, so weird-good – I saw Cokie touch herself to show me where.

"Decide to love –" she said.

We were leaving the building. We were walking down the hall, and we got outside in the tunnel... *and it wouldn't be any fun to go outside anymore, everybody'd have to stay inside, or live under the ground, it'd be the end of the world unless...*

(love me, love me, said cokie, love me!)

Rachel was talking to me, "You took me on back there. In a way I just want to stay at home, just be a girl with a disease. I'm scared, and when I get real scared, I flip. But when I felt that moving in me that day outside your house – that really did it. Then that man was there. He confirmed it. It was a miracle... My room began to have a smell of roses.....still does."

While she talked I saw on one of the doors, pencil markings, where the paint had chipped off. They looked familiar.

They looked like drawings of me and Shiny. I leaned my forehead there. I would get the pencil imprint on my head from touching it. I looked at my fingertips; they looked blue from the color of the old door, then I looked and I had blue all over me, and it was in the hallway, in smudges, and over on Rachel, on her white shirt, spilled on her.

"Let me out of here," I said, at the door. "Let me out, I'm sorry for what I did." I could hear nothing inside. I thought of those people back in their room, on the floor, but by now probably standing in the dim light of a lamp, or in the brighter light of an open refrigerator.

"I have to get away," I said, softly. Then I forgot: if I was somewhere trying to get out, or out somewhere, wanting to get in. I felt my fists held tight against the wooden door above my head; was I upside down? Then I smelled it again, like in the fit. Like mustard, and something old, and dead. It was a dead horse. It was tired of carrying me.

"What was that smell?" It was now the smell of the old damned shape, following close behind.

"I have it too," Rachel said. "It always happens. C'mon." I held onto this small, shaky girl who I said I loved, and who gave me her disease. I thought I could see in through her shirt to her back. I reached out to touch her there as she walked, between her narrow shoulders. I saw a story printed there. I saw her wriggling through the greened crawlspace –

When I touched her back, it made me feel upside down. She turned and put her head to my chest. The air in the tunnel had pieces in it. I avoided getting them in my mouth. I pressed her breasts against her chest. I hiked her up around me, and her legs got wrapped around to hold on.

"No," she said. She looked around. "Don't! Not yet. The baby's in there. I have to know that's how he was made. I have to. Don't!" So we held there. It seemed like a long time. I worried about the sky. It would be getting too windy outside and dark.

She said not to, but I found it, like a little door, with a latch. I pushed into her. It felt like mud. I went in deeper than I thought I could. Deeper until I cleared the mud and reached something I knew was colored red. She made a pointy face at me. Her eyes shut and opened.

I didn't care. I pushed in hard. I pulled out, and went back in her. Then, we were separate. She fought me, but she held on.

"I'm hurt," she said. "It hurt. I'm bleeding –"

She had a thin red line down there. Like cut fish water. I pulled out of her. It was a solid, deep red. The blood was coming out of her.

"Oh, God!" I said. I held her closer to me, then laid her out on the hallway floor. On her back with her legs held apart, the blood flowed out making a pool. She turned onto her side. Her stomach was moving in and out, her side so thin I could see her ribs. Her hips — I could've covered one with my hand. And there was all that red getting bigger.

"Help me," she said. "I'm losing the baby, and everything else. Look at all the blood. It'll kill me."

Rachel bled continents from her. I saw the old shape on the floor, then on the rug. 'The child is the shape,' I knew. 'It's followed me even this far. It made this happen.'

I saw three thin boards, loose ones, standing against the wall. They were painted. One was red. One was sky blue. The other one was yellow. They were the color of melted popsicles. Rachel watched them too.

I heard a familiar voice, "They are the Father, the Son, and the Holy Ghost."

"A piece of Heaven here, and a piece of Hell," I said to me. They were the colors on Shiny's face. They were her. I knew she put them there to help us. I looked at Rachel, her eyes getting bigger, her hair wetter, and her blood moving towards the boards. She watched me with her hands. She closed her eyes.

* * *

Then, I was awake. Rachel woke me. I rushed up towards something, some shape above me. It was me. I filled it in. There was a woman on the floor, asleep. In the other room was a man, sitting at a table still smoking a cigarette. Maybe that's all he did. There was a rope hanging from a pipe above our heads.

"God! Where are we? Where have we gotten to?"

"Let's go," she said. "You fell asleep."

"What –?" I said. "I don't know… I –"

"Let's just go –"

On the door to the room were the pencil drawings, childish ones. One drawing was of a horse. It had huge eyes, a deep, almost camel-like swayed back, and more than four legs. There were stick figures nearby, around it. There was a fish, too, with a knife stuck in it. It wasn't funny and it looked sad.

We were finally outside in the air. In me was the not-knowing what had really happened.

"My life's been bad," I said. "I wish we were somewhere else. I wish we were in that clearing place where I was once was with my family. It was a place for angels if there ever was one, but I don't know where it is."

"This is okay here. I have the chills," she said. "Look."

"No one's ever done what we've done, and what you did tonight at the jail."

"I don't know," I said. "I didn't do anything, but hope. I had an unbelievable dream, or something back there. I think my sister was there."

"I didn't sleep at all," she said. "I waited for you."

"I know why that woman hung herself," I said.

"She was unhappy?"

"Well, yeah, probably, but it's something else. The jerk of that rope, it's like when I used to drink."

"What do you mean?"

"It's like when I was normal, I was in touch with the regular place – the long haul – a sense of a beginning and an end. A sense of self, you know. To me, that's hard. It's like a demand, somehow, a burden to be here, and to feel.

"When I drank, it broke it up, into pieces. Interesting pieces, too – sometimes horrible, but still, there were such details that got so big." I thought back to the cats in the alleyway. They were with my drunken mind, weaving, and slanted, and safe.

"The details get clear, but the big picture is lost completely – it's like throwing away your life down a slow hole."

"She must've hated something," said Rachel.

"Yeah, well, she was probably sick of being sick. So that rope was a serious way out –"

"Of ending it –"

"Yeah," I said. "Faster than throwing it away slowly, but the same."

"He said he would get me, while you slept."

"He never will," I said.

We lay down for awhile, outside, not far from the old hotel, but far enough away. We stretched out on the ground, in the park, in the deep shadows where no one could ever see, and she spoke like a tin saxophone, small in her throat. She sang into my face. I put my hand into Rachel's back pocket and felt how she was there. Our legs lay out below us, so we put them into each other's.

I thought about my Grandfather's story. He was in me. 'Who was he: A man and horse in a wooden coffin together, so strange to me now.

'Shiny, what's happening to me?' I thought about her and the story about the wind. I lay down in the park with my epilepsy.

CHAPTER 28

"I used to have a little dog," I said. We sat up against the edge of the old gazebo. "I rescued him from the pound. He knew me, he knew I would get him the minute he saw me. He was in his own cage - like me. I called him Billy. He was really smart, and nice. He never barked, hardly, and he just slept when I did. He looked like a toy, a big one. He felt like a little lamb. He was a great puppy. He cut his eyes around so you could see the whites. He slept under the table. And he cried when I left him. I miss him."

"What happened to him?"

"I ate him —"

Rachel barked.

"I gave him away. I had a hard time taking care of him. He didn't understand the way I lived. He had to cry a lot."

"But he was a dog. You said he was good. —"

"He was. It was me. I was messed up. But you know, I loved him and it hurt to give him away. I sang him little songs, on the floor with him. '...you're a pretty nice boy...' I sang to his face."

"Is that what you'd do to me?"

"Yeah, I would. I'd sing a dog song to you. I'll kiss your great face."

"No — give me away?"

"I hope not. If I can keep you, right, if I can then I'm saved."

"I don't think I'm gonna have any more attacks," she told me.

"That'd be good," I said. "I think you're right. I guess we'll see... I'll probably have a heart attack."

"You won't."

I worried, though, I thought that I'd have her attacks from now on for her, but then, I would. I would. I touched her on the back, and I knew the shape was lurking nearby, desperate, with another story to tell, because it knew my dear, dead sister was nearby.

* * *

I saw her, my long-dead sister, Shiny, finally, on the street. She was sitting on a bench, by herself. Her feet were stretched out in front of her. I knew it was her.

On the bench directly across the street from her, sweet, strange-friend Rachel went and sat. Sometimes, I called her Ray.

I sat down by Shiny.

"It's you," I said. "Isn't it?"

"Yes," she said to me, "I saw you coming. I knew you'd be here, eventually."

I blew up inside my old heart. I might have had a hole blown out from me, the edges on it singed and gray.

I remembered her belt loops I once held, her cottons, and the colors she wore.

"You," I said. "Oh, look at you – Shiny –" I looked for the three stripes on her dear face.

"I remember you wanted those color stripes on your face," I said.

I was talking to my long-lost sister, Shiny-Elizabeth.

She laughed.

"You look the same," I told her. "You look how I think of

you, but a little older, and bigger."

"Carl. You've been to me like I've been to you, all this time. Do you know that?"

"No, I didn't – know that."

There was a streetlight down a short way, to see her by. She was still my sister, and she was here. The night felt good, it supported us, not hot, or cold, almost unnoticeable. I wrapped up in her. Rachel sat across from us. She made herself look smaller; she pulled up the collars of her shirt to her chin.

"The three of us," I said. "I wish we could have one season together, like this Fall. I want that with you, and with Rachel. That girl is Rachel Coyne, over there." Shiny nodded.

"I don't want to go back to what it was, to my life."

"No?"

"Without you. And where the hot sun shines," I said. "I like it when it's dark, and easy, and no one is around much. I don't like the sun out, in the day very much - I just want to sit around, with you, and know what we're feeling and thinking, without saying much. Just be there at nights."

"There are other kinds of light, that are maybe okay," she said. Her voice was one of them, on me. A small, warm flashlight touching my face like a small hand. There were lights in Shiny's chest, like small, crowded candles.

Her teeth flashed white in the semi-dark. Her eyes were brown, to my happiness. She had a few more lines near her eyes and mouth. I hardly noticed anything but just her being there on the bench. I wasn't so amazed to find her. I'd hoped we'd sit somewhere and talk. The triangle we were, in that distant living room, with our mother, where we were formed, so long ago, led to this place, a thin extension of it, nothing in-between but waiting room time.

I looked at Rachel, carrying a baby inside her, under her stomach where I had never really been. It had seemed so real each night with her. Once she'd been on both sides of a thick window at one time.

Everything was already foretold, so I watched.

"It is true about her, about Rachel," said Shiny. She started to point. "You'll probably have a child. It'll just be a child." She laughed, "but it might have something very different...."

I felt us on the bench; it began to hum.

"You know, I'm still back there," I said, "I'm still that kid, I'm always that same kid. I still look like him even, to me. All that time ago. Nothing has happened since then – I can't believe you're here now. Shiny, I became a monster –"

"Stop, Carl. I know, but time is not the same as you think. I'm waiting up for you. I'm saving you a place by me. There's no hurry. I'd forgive you, really, but truly there's nothing to forgive. We were children.

"We swim in the ponds in those mornings. That's enough. I feel so good to sit here with you. Look at my face – can't you tell?"

"I don't know what you are," I said, "now - or before. Were you just a sister, or were you more like a girl for me, you know, like a girlfriend, some kind of lover?

"You're now like everything you ever were – and every place -"

"Carl, we were all of that. I'm still me. I'm kind of like - I'm not sure really, either – but I'm just a little bit different, in a different place. But I want to tell you – we were not supposed to be separated, like we were, like we are. That's why it's been so close, and so strange. We were meant to be together and have love between us for a long time. That's what we want to do. What happened is a mistake. We were torn apart. And you knew that all along. That's why *Shiny* means so much –"

When she said her name like that, I saw the others around her. There was a group of people, some as children, around her, in a semi-circle at her end of the bench. They looked like they were a part of her. I could just make them out. They held close to each other in a light. They loved her very much. I looked to see her wrist where the tied string had once been so many years ago, and it made me want to cry, to know I hadn't done a thing since that time. I'd wasted my life without her.

Shiny had her hands at my face, at my eyes. She touched me. She was smiling hard, her whole face in it. She couldn't stop it.

"I know what you think. And, no you haven't wasted anything. How could you know what you've done? And now you're with her —"

She looked at Rachel. "She is an adoration. She is full of Grace. So, you have to forgive yourself now, of all the enemies inside of you. They can go away now. You can get past that day. And you know that I know. There are some hard things that have to be melted. They will be, I promise you."

Rachel sat watching us.

"I was taken away from you, maybe for you, somehow," she said. "So now, you won't fall down, anymore. Please don't."

She told me more, and her voice changed: "When I am seventeen, I'm running away from the life I had. I am running after a truck that drove by our house each morning. There's a ledge on the back of it and I chase it. I wear a coat and I carry a bag in my hand. I reach out and I grab a hold, and I ride. I want to get away. I want to look for my brother. I climb into the back of the truck through silver doors and I sit and I curl up in myself. Then, soon, I'm in a different place for a long time. I die, to the world I know. I cross over.

"I ascend in a milk truck accident. I'm a girl who is dying that day."

"You're here, now," I told her. "This is where we lived, in our hometown. I never left here." I was shaking on the bench with my sister.

"Shiny, do you remember a place, in the woods or somewhere, in a clearing - we were with Mom, and it was cool out and clear, where we slept in a house with feather beds, and you were so pretty – I can never figure out where that was?"

"That's where I am, much of the time, Carl, that's funny, that's a place where you and our mother are often. We're almost there now. You sort of come there and act funny, and then are gone. Sort of checking in on me there. It's a place that's always happening to us."

"You were like the green trees, and Mom looks tall and great there."

Then I felt a great rush of being at that wonderful place, the smell, the wind, the changes, and the girl I knew then as her. I closed my eyes with that, and in it I felt myself there alone. There may have been others there. I felt myself running headlong and fast, and hard and falling down and wanting. I was looking for Shiny, desperately, and in that I saw her lying down, face downward in a pond at the side of a road I didn't know. She wore a dark coat. I opened my eyes, and asked her about what I saw.

"It's me. I'm in a pool of water by the side of the road. I'm always there. And there's milk, a lot of broken bottles, and spilled milk in the water with me. I can see the very small waves in the white water. It's a big puddle really –" She laughed. "It's okay. I'm okay, you know.

"It's unexplainable to you. Everything happens all the time – now seems most alive is all, usually. It's a very big place, and I don't know much about it. Just know that I am with you."

"You look beautiful, lying down like that, just how you are. I'd rather look at you, even like that, than at anything else."

"But now you can. You can look around. Tonight's special for you, and for her," and Shiny nodded to Rachel who appeared to be sleep-watching. "You saw some things."

"I've aged," I said. "I worried I'd never see you ever again. That made me sad. After awhile I believed I never would."

Shiny put her arms out at me, spread them out. They

seemed to bring in everything I ever thought about, or knew of her.

I leaned into her. I buried my face in her clothes; she wore a coat, and had a soft shirt on underneath.

"I love you," I told her. "I love you."

"There's no one in this world that remembers me, Carl, or ever cared about me, but for you."

I smelled her, the same warm, and only home I knew. I felt her life, her heart, my sister. I held her close to me and closed my eyes. I drew her in, to last me forever.

I felt her gone, after awhile. She slipped away. I almost forgot it happened.

Shiny was going – she was just rounding the corner. I saw her wrist in my mind; I saw the colored string, pink now, dangling down about four inches. She hadn't been able to stop her face from smiling. And those other ones, they followed close to her. And another, greater something, watching.

She rounded the corner and was gone. She ascended to heaven in a milk truck, and I had run so hard, looking, and hadn't gone anywhere at all. I sat alone on my bench and over where Rachel was doing the same.

My mother had whispered behind the locked door of our childhood, *shiny, shiny, shiny apalaris…*

CHAPTER 29

Rachel said yes, she had seen someone and sometimes just me talking to myself. It scared her, she said.

"What'd she say to you?"

"She talked some about you. She said you were – special."

We walked along a dead street where no one much went ever. I wasn't sure about that night, about any of it.

Along the street we walked were the old, beat-up houses of the town, known to be that way by everybody. If you wanted to go crazy and tear up your house and pile it in the yard, this is where you moved. Most people just dropped their garbage out the window into the yards. I used to see a certain little man sitting with his head in his hands out on one of the stoops. He hated to live there. I saw him out in the rain one day. I looked for him now, but he wasn't there.

"Roan Street," I said.

"Yeah," said Rachel. "Isn't that a horse name?"

There was litter along the curbs, the tin cans with food still stuck in them that the cats got at – cigarette butts, wrappers, old paper stuff, beer cans, plastic throw away, and Cokie. Some of the town's ghosts were out. We saw her shadow first. She was walking along behind us. I saw three shadows by the street light.

"Hi," she said. We turned to her. "I followed you."

Her hair was cut, as if with dull, drunkard-held garden

shears. Her eyes looked dark-circled, and her body was swollen looking. She was still a child. And in her was a darkish appeal. She smiled sideways at me. She nodded to Rachel. She was a nineteenth century workhouse girl. I saw her hands held in front of her stomach. She had on an orange sweater.

We stood across from each other in the pools of light. There was the junk all around us.

"I followed you from near your house. It was a mistake – I mean an accident – to see you. I was out walking and I saw you."

"I figured I might see you." I said. "I thought about you, over at my house. I was just talking to my sister for awhile. I'm in jail – I mean I'm supposed to be there. I thought about you, before..."

"We had a fire, a while ago in my house," she said. "My Mom says I started it, but I never did. I was at home with my brother – I have no idea. We saw it burning the curtains. It lit up the whole room. It was running up 'em fast, too. We'd been watching TV, and I saw some weird shadows. That's why I look sort of bad."

"You look good, Cokie."

"Yeah? We ran in where it was on fire, and it just scared us so much, we stood and watched. Then we ran. We tried to put it out with glasses of water –

"So, they're all mad at me there. I stay away as much as I can – plus the house is all messed up."

"Cokie. When was that?"

We inched closer as we listened to her. I had to turn my head to hear her speak.

"About a week ago, I guess."

"This is Rachel," I said.

Cokie said her name. Rachel liked the word. She said she did.

"I guess we're hiding," I told her.

"I saw you go in that place, upstairs. I was scared to go in there. I would never go there."

"It was really weird," said Rachel.

"You were up there a long time," she said. Rachel looked at Cokie's mouth. I saw how she saw it. Her mouth was like a birthday cake and all the candles, pretty. She had the little fires on inside her. Maybe her hair got burned off in the house fire.

"We had to go there," I said. "There was some old stuff in there."

"I can't hardly go home anymore. But, like I said, it's okay. I put it all in a box. Like you. I put you in the box too."

We looked at her.

"My Dad died. He left me an empty box.

"He had a heart attack. He was pretty young, too. I always felt nervous with him.

"I got to be alone with him in his hospital room at the end for awhile, and I talked to him. He wasn't awake – he was unconscious – so I talked and talked. He was like a child, even younger than me. He was like a doll. I held his hand, and I talked. It broke my heart."

"I guess I thought the other man, with your mom, was your dad."

"No. He's my step-dad. In the hospital, my dad's eyes were closed. I talked to him close up, at his ear. He was mostly bald, he kept the hair he had real short – and it had grown out some. That really caught me. And it was white. I lifted his eyes so he would have to see me – so I would go inside his eyes and into his brain one last time. I tried to smile when I did that, in each one. And a couple of tears came out of his eyes. So, I don't know.

"And I keep it, here," she pointed at her heart, "...the box, so I can't lose it." She narrowed her eyes at me when she stopped.

When she talked, her mouth moved.

"You put me in there?" I asked her.

"Well, everything's in there."

"You were my sin," I told her. "Not you, but me." I remembered how it looked on her chest and raised up on her back.

"That's not true," she said. "That's just what you think. I used to think about you a lot, and feel sad; now I don't. We had fun.

"I wasn't doing good before. I have to trust the box."

"Would you forgive me, then -?"

Cokie looked inside.

"Will you stay at my house - while I'm gone?"

"Where you going?"

"I'm going back to jail – before it's dawn. I think I have to, now, to be able to get what I want." Rachel stood next to me. I knew it wasn't any surprise. She would be tired; she needed to be somewhere normal. She was too small.

"You know where the key is, in the back, you can just go there, tonight, and stay as much as you want to – use what ever you need. Use the backdoor – there's some police notice on the front. Pay no attention to it.

"Me and Ray might be having a baby, soon –" I said. I felt like I could not walk backwards, then, take one step back behind me or I would die.

"Didn't you just meet each other?"

"We met right before I went to jail – we're not sure we're having a baby – but Rachel thinks so, and I believe it."

"Well, I hope it won't be – anything like a problem for you." She said, "God Bless it, and you two. So, there are four of us here, I guess – that I didn't know about. I hope I get to see it, when it's born, when it arrives."

She twisted in her place. I heard her tennis shoes rub the street. She was like the best story to read.

Once she said she wanted me to call her, from wherever I was, wherever I got to - in the world. Please, just call me up, she said – no matter what. 'Cause I know you won't be with me.'

"I have to go," she said.

"Please don't be lonely -"

"I won't be."

"Go to my house - okay?"

"Okay."

We watched her go. She walked away from us, too soon. It would always be too soon. She was like night, in this town, the sweeter, painted part. She ... a barefoot girl on a dirt road. Her heels and toes were dark with the road, and her world.

I saw her disappear right before the first light could come. Part of me ran after her down the alleyway.

I saw her getting into my bed at home, making it be a good place, a light on, then off, and her fingers at the switch, seen by her for an instant, then disappearing like smoke.

"She's just a little girl," said Rachel. "She's different. Do you think you did something to her, not good?"

"I don't know. She's important. She was like my own child-hood."

We sat on the curb.

"She idolizes you," Rachel said.

"I don't know -"

"I idolized someone once," she said. "He was like you, in a way. I knew him all my life. He lived in the house behind ours. He was older, but nothing like you and Cokie. I followed him around, and watched him. Sometimes, I had little fits. I think he liked me cause of that. He liked to watch me. But he cared about me, too, I know.

"I took off my blouse with him once. I was about fourteen, when we were still living down in Georgia. He was seventeen.

"I remember him, in a yellow, dark hallway at my house. His name was Danny Paul. I wanted to, but I couldn't take off my blouse close to him. He had black hair, combed back. He was always gentle with me. I saw him smoking out near the backstop on the baseball field once when I walked by. He always saw me watching him. He burned down our trellis one summer with a cherry-bomb.

"He said to come closer, that I was a blur to him, a 'pretty blur,' he said. I slid the buttons on my blouse through the holes, one at a time. I was scared. I could feel my heart pounding behind each button, harder and harder. Then I had it undone. I just took it off. I didn't have much, there – of course. I felt available to him. I felt so little.

"He held my hands down. I remember feeling sort of protected by my hair. I straddled his lap, like a pony. I just sat there and put my arms around his neck and held him close to me. I could see out the hall window at a distance. I saw all the things I knew outside.

"That was really all that happened - but it was a lot to me...

"After that, I still saw him around, and when they played baseball. When we moved he said goodbye to me. The moving van was out at the house and he came over, to say goodbye."

* * *

We sat still, on the curb.

"Now it is almost light out," she said. "Are you going back?"

"Yeah, I think I am. I want to. I mean, I don't want to have to run away - do you?"

"No. I guess I don't. It's easier not to," she said.

"In a way, all we have to do is keep being like we are. We haven't really done anything wrong. I'm gonna let myself off the hook, for awhile." I felt the wide smile coming on. I was surely my sister's twin.

"When I was a little boy, I liked myself. It's like this thing we drew, in school, on the wall once, a long time ago - a big mural. We drew a big Christmas thing with colored chalk. I was on my knees on the floor to draw my part. It was a big desert scene with camels and the wise men and the star, a huge Star of Bethlehem. It's a clear memory, now. I liked that chalk. I feel chalky colored, to think of it. It was pure color. You could even breathe it in. After those days things turned harder. But I had Shiny…

"I believe that in a few months, if we do have a child, that it'll be great, like a perfect childhood. It'll be an ordinary miracle."

"People might think my Father did it, with you in jail, or somebody else."

"Let them."

"People might want to hurt the baby, if he's different. They won't want to hear about miracles -"

"No one needs to know about him - the beginning of him."

"How did it begin?" she asked me.

"I don't know."

"We might have to live different… maybe move from here."

"I've never really left this town," I said. "But, I could, if we had to."

"Yeah," she said to me.

"Eventually we'll have to prepare, to get ready to leave everywhere, when we die. I guess a shorter move we could do –" I smiled out in the air

"Will you still visit me when I go back?"

"Of course," said Rachel. "It'll be different now, though, after tonight. After those people at the hotel, and stuff. That was so strange, it was like we were all pretending.

"Look, there goes the trash truck," she said. "It's really close to dawn now."

"There's a family that runs that trash company," I told her. "They all work on the truck. There's a girl who does. When she walks she always watches the ground. And she stutters. I talked to her a few times. She said she stutters because of boredom. She said she started for fun, but now it's stuck, and she can't help it. The only thing clean on her was the whites of her eyes."

"Strange people are born in our town," she said to me. "They're like little tin people who live in a little tin house and ride on a trash truck made out of tin. There are little versions of them sold all over the country at gas stations, and stores, and the real ones live here in our town. And there are tin models of that weird hotel, and of those people, and there's even a little rope that comes with it. And of us...and of Shiny.

"You know how tin tastes, or certain metal - like tin foil, when you put it in your mouth? That's how that trash truck girl would taste to kiss her. That's how blood tastes. And our baby will be born here."

While Rachel talked like that, the light was coming up, growing on her face. It seemed funny that people could run and move, freely, without any wires or ropes holding them up, or motors. They were all made to run around from inside of them.

I started to disappear when the stars did. They faded away is all.

"I feel really happy now, for no reason," Rachel said. "The world got really little then, like there would hardly be any room except for a few people – just us – maybe three or four people, on a little piece of ground."

"That's little," I said.

I put my fingers up to my eye to look through them at Rachel. I did it, and then I looked over at the faint moon. It was low on the edge of the world, almost morning. It was like a toy.

"All this stuff," I said.

I walked with Rachel, towards her house, then up to it. I touched it. We said more things. I could see her face getting more clearly lit. She wasn't so small. It was easy to put my face against hers. I helped her go through her open window. The white curtains blew, and pushed in with her. I had my hands open and helping. I put them against her back pockets. Then she was in, and turned around, and watching me from it, walking away. It wasn't far to go for me. The last time I looked back, there was just a dark square in the side of a house.

When I walked back, I knew everyone else was somewhere other than with me. The world swooped down small again, and I had to watch where I put my feet. I went back into the jail, the same way I'd gotten out.

And there, Shiny, standing in front of me. In a line. There were other kids around. I held her belt loop. Some person asked her, if I was with her.

She said, "Yeah, he is.

I said, quietly, but she heard me, "Yes, I'm with her. Thank God."

ABOUT THE AUTHOR

RUDY WILSON is the author of three previous novels, THE RED TRUCK, A GIRL NAMED JESUS, and SONJA'S BLUE. He is the recipient of a CCLM-GE Award for fiction published in *The Paris Review*, an NEA Fellowship, and a Teaching-Writing Fellowship from the University of Iowa's Writers' Workshop, where he attended and taught. He has also taught at three other universities. He has published in many outstanding literary journals including *The Paris Review, The Indiana Review (3), Gordon Lish's Ouarterly, The Literarian*, and others, and has been nominated for a PUSHCART PRIZE for 2014. He is presently editing his new book, EXIT-ANGEL.

www.ingramcontent.com/pod-product-compliance
Lightning Source LLC
Chambersburg PA
CBHW031228260626
47169CB00007B/2199